Regrowth

Robbie Dorman

Regrowth by Robbie Dorman

www.robbiedorman.com

ISBN-13: 978-1-7336388-6-9

Cover design by Bukovero

For Smokey.

1

The last thing Jon expected was a phone call from the richest man on Earth.

He answered groggily, not recognizing the number, his brain still half asleep.

"Hello?" he asked.

"Did I wake you, Jon?" asked the voice, one that Jon had heard before, but only on the news. He recognized it and didn't.

"Who is this?" asked Jon.

"This is Eaton Shaw," said the voice. "My assistant has tried to contact you for a week, Jon. Thought I'd reach out personally."

The name Eaton Shaw pushed out most of his dreariness. He blinked his eyes and wiped them with his free hand. Eaton Shaw? That was impossible. He suddenly had the same feeling in his gut he would get in elementary school, when he would disappoint a teacher, or forget to do his homework.

Technology magnate Eaton Shaw, the man who made money when anything was bought or sold on the internet, was talking to *him*.

"It's been a rough week," said Jon, the only excuse he could muster. And it had been. To be fair, it'd been a rough few months, but this week had been harder than most. They had locked down his lab, leaving him with nowhere to work. He'd been sleeping there as well.

"I imagine it has," said Shaw. "My eyes and ears tell me it's hard out there." Shaw paused, took a breath. "I don't have much time, Jon, so let me get straight to it. I need your help."

"Help with what?" asked Jon.

"I have a lab, Jon. I want you there. I want your research there."

"My research?" asked Jon. "Why me?"

"Because it could change the world, Jon. You're a part of a larger whole. The world is ending, Doctor, and I don't intend to quietly slip into the night. If we are going to go out, I mean to go out fighting. And not with soldiers and bombs, but with science and intelligence. I have been a fool for waiting this long, but it is time to pull the ripcord."

Jon looked out his window into the early morning light. The roads were empty and had been for days. The president had declared martial law. But only two days ago, rioters had flooded the streets, and Jon had barricaded his door, unsure of what else to do. His food was running low, and he'd have to go to the grocery store at some point. Word was they still had milk, but he was afraid. He'd been surviving on rice and beans for days.

"So what do you say?" asked Shaw.

"Where is this lab?" asked Jon.

"It's a secret," said Shaw. "Very few know the location. To protect you, and it, from outside influence. But it's fully stocked, and nothing is outside my grasp. You'll have whatever you need, whatever resources you require."

Jon thought to his lab, which he so coveted, running on decade old computers and borrowed equipment. Which was now barred from him, and would be for the foreseeable future.

"When do you need an answer by?"

"I have to be off this call in three minutes," said Shaw. "So by then."

Jon looked outside again, reflexively.

"What about my family?" he asked.

"I was under the impression you lived alone," said Shaw.

"I do," said Jon. "But I still want to give them the chance."

"We have living quarters and support systems in place for any family of team members," said Shaw. "If they wish to come, they may."

"Then I'm in," said Jon.

"Good," said Shaw, his voice showing happiness for the first time. "I'll have you picked up."

"When?" asked Jon.

"Within an hour," said Shaw. "They're already on their way. You'll have to forgive me, Jon, but I need to go. I'll see you when you arrive."

And then the call ended. Jon took a deep breath and got out of bed. He shaved, showered, and quickly threw together all his clothes into a suitcase. It wasn't hard, there wasn't much.

His research. It was in piles of papers in boxes, sitting in the corner of his living room and on an assortment of thumb drives, all in a shoebox. He piled them up. He would need it all.

All the while his guts ached, full of nerves and anxiety. The car would be here soon, and he couldn't put it off anymore. He found his cell phone and called Maya. He hadn't talked to her in months. Not after he had gotten into the screaming match with Tommy.

"Hello?" she answered.

"Hey, Maya," said Jon. "It's me."

"Jon," she said. Her voice was measured. It always had been. At least until it wasn't.

"How are you both?" he asked.

"We're doing okay," said Maya. "All things considered. Tommy is still asleep. I'm leaving for my next shift in a couple hours. Are you okay?"

"I'm fine," said Jon. "That's why I'm calling. They shut down my lab."

"Well, you're not exactly essential business," said Maya. "Not with everything going on."

"No, probably not," said Jon. "I have a question for you."

Jon heard her take a deep breath.

"Jon, whatever you're thinking, now is not a good time. I don't think Tommy has—"

"It's not that, Maya. I just got off the phone with Eaton Shaw."

"Wait, what? *The* Eaton Shaw?" asked Maya.

"Yes," said Jon. "The one and only. He's running a lab. Inviting the best and brightest, is what he said. And for some reason, that includes me."

"Well, congrats," said Maya. "That's kind of crazy."

"I—yes, there's literally a car on the way now to pick me up," said Jon. "But that's not it. He said I can bring my family along. I don't know where it is, but it's safe, it's protected, and we'll be taken care of while we're there."

"Jon—"

"Do you want to come with me? You and Tommy? I know that I've been distant lately, and that Tommy still probably resents me—"

"Jon—"

"And this isn't an attempt for us to get back together. I just want you both to be safe. Shaw talked about his resources, and it has to be safer than where we are now. It's getting worse every day, and I don't know how long we'll have any semblance of order, I can't even get groceries, I can't imagine what it's like at the hospital—"

"Jon. Take a breath," said Maya. Jon paused, realizing he hadn't stopped talking since she had answered.

"Where is this lab?" asked Maya.

"I don't know," said Jon. "Shaw wouldn't tell me. He's keeping it isolated away from everything."

There was a long pause, and Jon heard Tommy's voice on the other end. Maya talked to him off the phone, and Jon only heard their muffled back and forth.

"But it's safe there?" asked Maya.

"It's run by Eaton Shaw," said Jon. "The richest man on Earth. He said that we will save the world. So I imagine it's impregnable."

Another long pause.

"I can't go," said Maya. An ache entered Jon's heart and silence hung between them. "I'm glad that you're a part of it, but my work is out here. I can't abandon my patients. They need me now more than ever. Even if it's in my best interests to go with you."

"Maya—"

"But take Tommy," she said.

"Without you?" he asked, and he could hear her breath catch in her throat.

"Yes," she said, finally. "I don't know what's going to happen out here. But his safety is more important than anything."

Jon said nothing, his mind rolling over everything that the word *anything* contained. It contained the entirety of his ex-wife.

"Will he agree to it?" asked Jon. Tommy was 14, and both him and Maya had largely agreed that he was old enough to make a lot of decisions on his own.

"No," said Maya. "But this one isn't in his hands. It's in ours. He'll be ready to go by the time you get here. Will they have room for his wheelchair?"

"I don't know," said Jon. "We can improvise if we have to. Shaw can afford a new wheelchair."

"I guess that's true," said Maya.

His phone buzzed with a text message. He looked at it.

Car outside for you, hired by Mr. Shaw.

"They're here," said Jon. "I've got to go. We'll be there soon."

"See you soon," said Maya, and the call ended.

Jon grabbed a suitcase and a box of notebooks and went downstairs, past all his neighbors. A big black SUV was parked at the curb, and as he approached, a man in a suit and dark sunglasses got out of the vehicle.

"Mr. Matthews?" asked the man.

"Yes," said Jon.

"Let me help you with those," he said.

"There's more upstairs," said Jon. "And my son is in a wheelchair. Will there be room?"

The man didn't skip a beat. "I'll find it."

Jon went back and grabbed more boxes, stacking them high in his arms. He made one more trip, offloading it to the man.

"That's everything," said Jon.

"Good, let's go," said the man. "You should sit in the middle seats. They're the safest." He opened up the side door of the SUV and gestured for Jon to get in.

"Are we expecting trouble?" asked Jon. Another man wearing the same as the first sat in the driver's seat. He nodded at Jon as he sat down.

"Better safe than sorry," said the first, closing the door and getting back in.

"We're picking up your wife and son as well?" asked the navigator.

"Ex-wife. And she's staying. Only my son."

"What's the address?"

Jon gave it to them, and the navigator typed it into the GPS console. They were on their way.

Jon didn't know what to say, but neither of the men spoke. The SUV was gigantic, the largest vehicle Jon had ever been in. He felt a headache coming on, his body reacting to not getting his morning coffee. He'd be hungry within an hour, and he realized he didn't know how long this journey would take. How far was this place from New York?

"Do you know where I'm going?" asked Jon.

"We're taking you to Mr. Shaw's private jetway," said the navigator. "But we don't know where you're heading after that."

"I guess I'll be flying, then," said Jon. "Do you guys do this a lot?"

"We do whatever Mr. Shaw asks us to," said the driver, the first thing he'd said.

"That sounds ominous," said Jon. Neither of them answered, maybe because it wasn't a question. But it made Jon realize how vulnerable he was.

Within ten minutes they were at Maya's apartment, only a few neighborhoods over. She had wanted Tommy to stay in the same school district. And make it easy for Jon to see him. That hadn't lasted.

He texted her. *We're downstairs.*

Jon got out and waited by the car, alongside the navigator. Maya came out a couple minutes later, pushing Tommy in his wheelchair. Both of their faces were red from crying. Tommy's eyes were still wet. Maya's expression was both hard and soft, doing her best to maintain strength for her son.

Jon tried to read his son's face, but he couldn't. Jon crouched in front of Tommy and looked him in the eye. Tommy avoided eye contact, but finally gave in, a mixture of anger, sadness, and frustration all mired together.

"I know this was sudden," said Jon. "It was sudden for me too. I don't need you to like this, okay, but I just want you to know I'm trying my best. We're trying our best, and I love you." He looked at Tommy, and Tommy finally nodded in acceptance, trying to not cry anymore.

Jon hugged him, and Tommy squeezed back for what it was worth. Jon stood back up and looked to Maya. He went to her and hugged her. She squeezed him hard.

"Take care of him," said Maya.

"I don't know if we'll be able to reach you," said Jon. "I don't know anything. But I won't let anything happen to him. Be careful out here."

"I'll do what I can," said Maya. "Let me say goodbye."

Jon backed up, and Maya hugged Tommy. She whispered to him, and Tommy nodded, saying something in return. He started crying again. They held an embrace, and then Maya let go. Tommy wiped away his tears.

"Let's get you in the truck," said Jon. Tommy reached out, a familiar movement, and Jon grabbed him, his missing lower legs making him weigh less. Jon held him and the navigator opened up the door, and Jon placed Tommy inside. Maya folded up the wheelchair, and the navigator put it in the back.

Maya stood there while they closed the door. She waved as they drove away.

"Where are we headed, Dad?" asked Tommy.

"To a private airport," said Jon.

"Yeah, but where after that?"

"I don't know," said Jon.

They arrived at the exclusive jetway within an hour, a jet already sitting on the runway. A woman in a business suit waited near the plane. The two men from the car quickly took all the luggage alongside Jon's research and loaded it onto the jet, before returning to the car and driving away.

"Jon?" asked the woman. "And Tommy?"

"Yes," said Jon.

"Hello, I'm Nancy" she said, extending a hand. "Are you ready to go?"

"I mean, sure," said Jon.

"Then follow me," said Nancy, and walked toward the plane. Jon pushed Tommy's wheelchair. "I apologize, but we do not have a ramp for the chair."

"I'll carry it up," said Jon.

"Are you sure? I can—"

"I'll do it," said Jon.

The jet sat alone on the runway. The actual airport was quiet. Jon knew air travel had largely been shut down, but he guessed the normal rules don't apply to billionaires. They boarded the plane, Jon carrying Tommy aboard, and then carrying his wheelchair.

The plane inside was spacious. Nancy helped them to their seats.

"Can I ask where we're headed?" asked Jon.

"You can ask," said Nancy.

"But you won't answer," said Jon.

"Correct," said Nancy. "But I can tell you the flight will take about 5 hours."

"And there's no windows on this plane," said Jon.

"Correct," said Nancy, smiling. "And you will both be blindfolded once we arrive at the facility until you are safely inside."

"I guess Mr. Shaw is serious about keeping the location secret," said Jon.

"He's gone to great lengths to protect it," said Nancy.

"But you know where it is," said Jon. "And so do the pilots."

"It's not about total information control," said Nancy. "That's impossible. It's about reasonable levels of oversight. I would buckle up. We're about to take off."

Jon buckled his seatbelt. Tommy hadn't said a word since he'd gotten on the jet. He was studying the interior.

They took off, the departure smooth, and the plane reached cruising altitude within twenty minutes.

Nancy brought them sandwiches and drinks, and then settled in her own seat, popping open a laptop.

"How are you doing?" asked Jon quietly.

Tommy looked at him.

"I'm okay," he said. "I miss Mom."

"I know," said Jon. "But she wants to make sure you're taken care of. That's why you're here."

"I know that," said Tommy. "It doesn't make it any easier. We're going to go back, right?"

"Yes, yes," said Jon. "Mr. Shaw wants to change the world. He wants to fix things."

Tommy looked away at that, and Jon couldn't help but look at what remained of Tommy's legs. Thoughts flashed through his mind of the night he lost them.

"You trust him?" asked Tommy.

"I don't know," said Jon. "I believe what he says."

Tommy said nothing else, just opened up his backpack and pulled out a tablet, and plugged in some earbuds.

Guess the conversation is over.

Jon pulled open his own bag and took a tattered paperback out, and read. He picked at his sandwich.

The plane ride passed quickly enough. It almost startled him when Nancy told them they were descending.

"That was fast," said Jon.

They were on the ground in no time. Jon didn't know how to feel. A part of him was anxious, a gnawing deep worry that he couldn't rationalize away. Another was excited. Thrilled. He would get a chance to do science again. To research again, and not in some misbegotten third-rate lab.

The plane landed with a soft thud and taxied for a few minutes before coming to a stop. Nancy was ready with two blindfolds.

"Don't worry about your things," she said. "We'll have someone take them to your quarters. Tommy, do you like your wheelchair?"

"I mean, it's okay," he said. "Why?"

"Do you want to keep it? Or would you prefer a new one?" asked Nancy.

Tommy eyed her, thinking. "I'll keep it, for now."

"Fair enough," she said. "Ready for your blindfolds?"

"Ready as we'll ever be," said Jon, after exchanging a look with Tommy.

Nancy nodded and handed them over. "No peeking," she said.

Jon looked at the blindfold. They were more like goggles. He didn't know how anyone would see out of them.

"Will you be going with us?" asked Jon, straightening the strap of the blindfold.

"No," said Nancy, with a smile. "You won't see me again."

Jon glanced at her and then slipped on the blindfold. "Nice meeting you, then."

"Good luck," she said, and within a minute there were hands leading them away, carrying Tommy, placing him in his wheelchair.

It felt cool outside, especially cool for the summer, but

Jon didn't know what that meant. He didn't bother asking questions, because he knew he wouldn't get any answers. His guts ached in turmoil. He wanted desperately to rip off the blindfold, to see where they were, but he imagined that would end with him on a trip back to New York.

Or worse.

Jon hadn't thought about the other side of betraying the secrets of Shaw's lab, but all those thoughts rolled through his mind in a flood, and his vulnerability was his first thought, of Tommy's vulnerability, of what would happen if something happened to him now, leaving Tommy alone, but then the chill went away, and the hands guiding him were gone, and a minute passed, and he felt a slight falling sensation.

We're in an elevator. We're going down.

Time passed, but he didn't know how much. How fast were they falling? The lab was underground. But how far? A sudden voice pulled him out of his thoughts.

"You can take off the blindfolds," said a woman's voice.

Jon removed his, and he looked to see Tommy do the same.

A young woman stood in front of him. She was blond, with close cropped hair. Petite, just over five feet tall.

"Jon, Tommy," she said. "I'm Sabrina. Mr. Shaw's personal assistant."

They stood in an elevator, and Jon went behind Tommy, pushing him into a small room with carpeted floors and soft beige walls. It looked like a doctor's office. Another elevator door stood behind Sabrina.

She smiled, extending a hand, first to Jon, and then to Tommy. They both shook it.

"You're now standing in the FUTURE lab," she said. "Welcome."

2

"The Future Lab?" asked Jon.

"Yes," said Sabrina. "All capitals, FUTURE."

"What does it stand for?" asked Jon.

Sabrina smiled. "Everyone asks. It doesn't stand for anything."

"Then why—"

"Why capitalize?" asked Sabrina. "Because perception is reality, Dr. Matthews. And we're creating the future here, first and foremost. Follow me."

She turned without a pause and entered the elevator behind her, the doors opening as she approached. Jon pushed Tommy in. It was all stainless steel, with no discernible buttons. It felt like they were inside a bullet.

The doors closed.

"No buttons?" asked Jon, finally.

"Nadia, request systems level, please," said Sabrina, and then the tube moved downward. "Nadia is our facility admin."

"Is she—is she an AI?" asked Jon.

"No," said a voice from around them. "Just a person."

"Nadia typically won't answer," said Sabrina. "She has a very busy day. And Mr. Shaw doesn't trust AIs to do anything a human can do."

"Is she always listening?" asked Jon.

"Usually not," said Sabrina. "But she is always watching. There are cameras everywhere, aside from private quarters."

"Creepy," said Jon.

"You don't think about it after a while," said Sabrina.

The elevator stopped, and the doors opposite the ones they came in opened. Sabrina stepped out, and Jon followed with Tommy, stepping out into a field of glass. Glass tiles lined the floor, and dozens of rooms were segmented with frosted glass walls. Hallways criss-crossed back and forth, and a few people hustled about. As someone opened a door, the glass de-frosted, and the room became visible.

"Wow," said Jon.

"This is the Systems level," said Sabrina. "Mr. Shaw organized the FUTURE lab around four pillars. Systems, Problem Solving, Energy, and Medicine. Each has their own floor, their own lab."

They walked down the central hallway, and Jon peered down each cross-secting hallway as they went. They reached a room at the far end of the hall, the doors already open. A bald man of average height sat behind a gray desk, the top of it occupied by three monitors. He looked up as they approached.

"Ah, Sabrina," he said. "A new arrival."

"Yes," she said. "Paul, this is Jon and Tommy. Jon will be working in Medicine. Jon, Tommy, this is Paul Hicks. Admin for the Systems pillar."

Jon extended his hand, and Paul waved him off.

"Ah, we don't shake hands," said Paul. "But it is nice to meet you. You'll be in Medicine, right?"

"Yes," said Jon. "I assume, at least."

"You're in good hands with Donald," said Paul. "I've got to get back to work. Good luck." And then he was looking at his screens again, his eyes darting between the different monitors. Sabrina led them back out.

"Can I ask what exactly does Systems pertain to?" asked Jon, as they returned to the elevator.

"It's complicated," said Sabrina. "The way it was explained to me is macro to micro examination of how we live and survive. Broadly, across all humanity, how do governments work, how do different systems of cultures interact. Basically, trying to figure out to operate humankind better."

"That sounds complex," said Jon. "And Paul is in charge of all that?"

"Sort of," said Sabrina. "He's an admin. Not a doctor. He manages the teams here, gets them the resources they need, and tries to keep them focused. He doesn't do the research work himself. Mr. Shaw thought it was best to keep the labor divided that way. And that is congruent over all four pillars."

They were back in the elevator, and Energy was next. The labs looked largely the same. The only difference was the blast shielding present around multiple sections of the Energy lab.

They walked in and met with Jordan King, who barely had the time to say hello before he rushed off.

"Energy probably is self-explanatory, but of all the needs of humanity, solving our energy crisis would immediately change the scope of civilization."

Jon only half listened to Sabrina now, because his eyes had caught sight of a woman in a lab coat, her curly black hair softly bobbing as she walked. It was an absent-minded look, but she turned and caught his eyes in hers, just for a moment, and then he broke eye contact, and they kept walking.

Back to the elevator, and Problem Solving was next. Cynthia Samuels wasn't in her office, and Sabrina couldn't find her, so Jon didn't get an introduction.

"Problem Solving seems kind of vague," said Jon.

"Purposefully vague," said Sabrina.

"I don't get it," said Tommy. He had said little since they'd left the plane, but he was opening up.

"Well, certain fields have intrinsic advantages to mankind. Medicine, Energy. Both easily contained under their own umbrellas. But for other problems, their solutions cover many fields. Reversing climate change or creating corn that can grow anywhere. Targeted teams, trying to solve big problems."

"So, literally, problem solving," said Jon.

"Yes," said Sabrina. "But you'll find that none of our teams operate on an island. Even the pillars do not operate alone. Let's say a problem solving team needs an efficient energy solution as part of their research. They can go to Energy for it. That is a large part of each admin's responsibility. Enable cross organization cooperation."

All of this was coming in a whirl, and they continued their tour, going to the last pillar, Medicine, Jon's future home.

"And this is where you'll be working," said Sabrina, as they walked through a similar setup, with frosted glass rooms. The open labs featured a lot more stainless steel, and people hustled around, much like the other floors. It smelled different on this floor, however. After a while, you got used to it, the scent of disinfectant mixed with medicine mixed with human. The smell of hospitals. But being without it for weeks, Jon noticed it now. The smell of the erasure of blood.

They walked to the office in a similar place as the other pillars. The doors stood open, with a small man standing behind a standing desk, four monitors, plus two tablets on multiple stands around him, a minimalist wireless keyboard and mouse on the surface.

"Donald?" asked Sabrina.

"Oh, hello," said Donald, coming around from behind the desk. Jon could see him well now, with large glasses covering his small face, his hair kept trim and unobtrusive. Everything about him seemed to keep him small.

"This is Jon Matthews, and his son Tommy. Jon, Tommy, this is Donald Baskins, admin of the Medicine pillar."

Jon extended a hand again, before realizing himself and pulling it back.

"It's hard to get used to," said Donald. "But you'll adjust. I want to welcome you to my team, Jon."

"Thanks," said Jon. "This place is impressive."

"It is something, isn't it?" asked Donald. "But all in the service of science. Of *fast* science."

Jon thought to ask about that, but put it off until later.

The day had been a whirlwind, and he had lost track of time. He hadn't spotted any clocks inside the facility.

"I'm excited to get working," said Jon.

"We're still setting up your workspace," said Donald. "Your equipment is coming in as we speak. As well as your assistant."

"Assistant?" asked Jon. He'd never had one.

"Yes, brilliant young woman," said Donald. "She should be an asset. You'll meet her tomorrow. And I've looked over your research. Fascinating stuff. Do you really think it's possible? Limb regeneration, in humans?"

Jon looked to Donald, and saw Donald's eyes flit to Tommy, before going back to Jon.

"Yes," said Jon. "I do. We're closer than we've ever been. It's within our reach. And it's not just limbs. It's any kind of trauma."

Donald nodded. "You'll have your opportunity. Mr. Shaw has given me the green light to acquire anything you need. But we can go over that tomorrow."

"About that," said Jon, looking to Donald, and then Sabrina. "When is that, exactly? I haven't seen any clocks."

"We operate on our own clock," said Sabrina. "It will require some adjustment, on your part. But you'll be fine after a good night's sleep."

"Then tomorrow?" asked Jon.

"Tomorrow," said Donald. "We'll have everything ready for you."

They left then, back to the elevator. As they walked, they passed a lab with an open door, and Jon glanced inside. Dark eyes met his gaze, owned by an enormous man with a buzz cut. He glared at Jon, and Jon averted his eyes. He felt the anger in his stare.

And then they were back in the elevator.

"Is that everything?" asked Jon.

"Well, not quite," said Sabrina. "The facility is quite extensive, with multiple support levels, but you'll most likely never see them. We have whole teams of people who clean, who cook, and places to house them. But we keep the groups largely segmented."

"Okay, is that the last of the labs?" asked Jon.

"All but one," said Sabrina. "But we won't be going there today."

"Why?" asked Jon.

"You haven't earned it," said Sabrina, her tone serious.

"What does that mean?" asked Jon.

"I'm sorry," said Sabrina. "It's always the way Mr. Shaw phrases it, and it's rubbed off on me. The last lab is the special projects lab."

"Aren't all these special projects? Isn't that the point of this whole thing?" asked Jon.

"Well, yes," said Sabrina. "But it's where you go when you graduate. Anything Mr. Shaw wants to earmark, to focus on, gets moved there. It's for things ready for implementation, more or less. Where they get their finishing touches. Where we prepare them before we use them in the world."

"But we can't see them?" asked Jon.

"No," said Sabrina. "Again, segmentation. Mr. Shaw is readily aware of the dangers of sabotage, of theft. When something is so close to being useful, it's more dangerous even then. So the dark lab has another set of lock and keys protecting it."

"The dark lab?" asked Jon.

"Another name for it," said Sabrina. "Just don't use it around Mr. Shaw. He doesn't like the name."

"Are you ready to see your quarters?" asked Sabrina.

"Sure," said Jon. "I could use a breather."

"Nadia, request residential level, Jon Matthews," said Sabrina, and the elevator moved again. It stayed in transit for longer this time. Jon imagined the metal tube moving far down into the earth, dozens of stories, until it slowed and stopped. The doors opened.

"Each residential level is limited to forty families," said Sabrina. "Simply state what I did in any elevator, and it will get you here. Follow me."

There was no sign of glass here. It looked similar to a hotel hallway, with neutral colors and carpeting. But it reminded him of something else even stronger.

"This looks like—like Star Trek," said Jon.

"Yeah," said Tommy. "It looks like Next Gen."

Jon remembered sitting on the couch with Tommy, before the accident, watching Star Trek with him.

"It is intentional," said Sabrina. "Mr. Shaw is a fan and patterned a lot of the living spaces after it." They went down the corridor, passing a few dozen doors, each with a nameplate next to it. Sabrina came to a stop in front of one, finally.

"Jon, simply stand in front of the door," she said. Jon stepped up, and stood there, and a few seconds later, the door slid to the side.

"Tommy, it will work for you as well. No one else can gain entry. Please, go inside."

Jon pushed Tommy in, curious as to what their living situation would be in this new place.

"It's huge," said Tommy.

Jon had expected quarters like in a submarine, with cramped space. But their apartment was enormous. The door opened into a small foyer which then transitioned into a massive living area, with a giant flat screen television. Jon could see the kitchen beyond, big as well.

"You each have a bedroom and a bathroom," said Sabrina. "Each is catered to your needs. Your kitchen is fully stocked with essentials, and if you want anything, call operations and they will do their best to get you it. Not just food. Anything."

"Do we have internet?" asked Tommy. It was a good question.

"Of a sort," said Sabrina. "As I've said, Mr. Shaw is highly guarded about the secrecy of this place, but working without the internet is nigh impossible. So he built his own."

"Doesn't that defeat the purpose?" asked Tommy.

"You'll still have access to most websites," said Sabrina. "But there are security protocols in place for all connected devices. And everything you do will be monitored. But unless you're trying to leak secrets, I wouldn't worry about anyone stopping you. You'll also find your cell phones and tablets functionally useless. But you'll notice new devices in your rooms, which can be catered to your whims."

"Can we call outside?" asked Jon.

Sabrina paused. "You'll have to speak to Mr. Shaw about that. It's on a case-by-case basis."

Jon wanted to argue with her, but knew it would do no good. He would talk to Mr. Shaw, like she said.

"How does it look, Tommy?" asked Jon.

Tommy wheeled himself farther into the living room.

"Do you have video games?" asked Tommy.

"Yes," said Sabrina. "Call operations. The numbers are already on the devices in your room. They'll deliver anything you need."

Tommy looked to Jon. "It's a start," he said.

"Speaking of Mr. Shaw, when do I meet him?" asked Jon.

Sabrina opened a tablet and flicked the screen to the left multiple times.

"Right now, if you're ready."

3

He had forgotten. Jon had known, he knew it at some point, but it had slipped his mind.

But that knowledge came flooding back when he met Eaton Shaw, and Shaw extended his right hand for a handshake.

Eaton Shaw didn't have a right hand, or a right arm, for that matter. The distant headlines flashed through Jon's mind:

Billionaire in terrible accident
World's richest man feared dead
Shaw survives; loses arm

He had forgotten, but the stainless steel prosthetic that reached for a handshake reminded him. Jon didn't hesitate, reaching out and shaking. The grip was cold and firm, and he felt a strength behind that grip that could have crushed his hand.

"Nice to meet you, face to face, Jon," said Shaw, smiling. He had come out from behind his massive desk, solid, made from a redwood that probably cost more than Jon's whole life. Shaw was a few inches taller than him, his hair cut in tight lines on his head. Jon had heard the rumors about hair plugs, but tried not to study Shaw's hairline.

He couldn't help but look at Shaw's face, and noted the strange plasticity to it, and despite Shaw's money, the signs of plastic surgery were hard to miss. He didn't know Shaw's age, and it was impossible to tell from looking at him.

Jon smiled back. "Nice to meet you too, Mr. Shaw. I thought we didn't shake hands down here."

"The rules don't apply to me," said Shaw. "For multiple reasons. You may go, Sabrina. Don't let me keep you from your work." Sabrina smiled and was gone, out of Shaw's enormous office. It shared similarities with his apartment, with curved surfaces, neutral colors, and aesthetics straight from older Star Trek. There was a bar set up on one side, although everything was put away. Shaw's desk was empty, a vast landscape of clean red. "Please." Shaw gestured to a seat, and he returned to the massive chair that sat behind it. Jon felt like he was on a talk show. Shaw sat above him, and Jon had to cast his gaze at a slightly upward angle to meet his eyes.

"How was the flight?" asked Shaw.

"Comfortable enough," said Jon. "Sudden, but I feel like that's partially my fault. I hadn't checked my email in weeks."

"They are shutting down labs all over the world," said Shaw. "Just as we need them most. Foolish. It's part of the reason this place exists. To provide a home for the homeless, so to speak."

"Thank you for this opportunity," said Jon. "I'm glad to just be working again."

"No, thank you for coming here, Jon," said Shaw. "I've had my eye on you for a while."

"Really?" asked Jon.

"Yes," said Shaw. "Some are obvious reasons. Others are not. Have you heard of the term traumatropism?"

"Honestly, no," said Jon. "Although it feels like I should have."

"There's no shame in not knowing," said Shaw. "Especially when it's outside your field, technically. It's from botany, from plants. It's when a plant or tree regrows after catastrophic damage. After being struck by lightning, for example."

"Ah, that makes sense," said Jon.

"The tree will survive, despite being nearly cleaved in half. It will regrow from the damage, and live, perhaps for hundreds of years, but the evidence of the damage is ever there. The tree will grow, sometimes to huge size, even after being nearly rent in half, or burning from the inside. The signs of the trauma are always there. It's something that's always fascinated me. The Hibakujumoku as well."

"The what?" asked Jon.

"Hibakujumoku. It's Japanese," said Shaw. "Bombed trees, literally. They are trees that survived the atomic bombs of Hiroshima and Nagasaki. They are cataloged. I've visited all of them. The ones on record, at least."

"Never heard of it," said Jon.

"Visiting them is powerful," said Shaw. "It was one of the

first things I did after I recovered from my accident. Reminded me of the power of perseverance. Something the accident challenged in me. There is a particular tree, in Hiroshima. The bomb, it ripped it apart. A massive trunk, torn into five parts. Still together at the roots, still alive, but blown apart by the incredible force of the atomic bomb. When people returned to the city, they found it in this state. Do you know what they did?"

"No," said Jon, shaking his head.

"They found rope," said Shaw. "And they wrapped that rope around the pieces of the trunk, and forced them together, and the tree lived. But as it aged, the five separate pieces of the trunk grew upward, with more and more branches, thicker and heavier over the years. The tree still stands, with rope still holding that trunk together. Now what do you think would happen if they took off that rope?"

"I don't know," said Jon. "I imagine the tree would die."

"It would split itself apart," said Shaw. "The weight of the tree itself would kill it, without the rope supporting it."

As he spoke, the fingers of his prosthetic arm bent and flexed, and Jon couldn't help but look at them, watching them bend and move back and forth, back and forth.

"You'll have to forgive me," said Shaw. "It's reflex, at this point. The arm—it requires constant physical reinforcement. I almost never stop using it."

"I'm sorry," said Jon.

"It's quite alright," said Shaw. "It's one of a kind, but it's an enemy of your work."

"I'm not opposed to prosthetics," said Jon.

"This arm," said Shaw, "is rope. It is technology. More advanced, but still *rope*."

"In a perfect world, we wouldn't need them."

Shaw smiled again. "Ah, beautiful. A perfect world. We are on the same wavelength, Jon. Because that is what I'm striving for. A better place, for all of us. And I think your work can be a part of it. Because despite the fact that we are deep beneath the earth, I still have eyes and ears open up top, and it's not looking good."

"It's hard to get a complete picture," said Jon. "As one person. It's tough to watch the news and know what to believe."

"My information is unfiltered," said Shaw. "And multiple man-made crises are coming to a head, all at the same time. Frankly, humanity cannot persist at this rate. The dangers are escalating, and soon we will be at the point of no return, at least on a human timescale. Much faster than many anticipate." Jon thought to Maya, still up there, struggling. He tried to push it out of his mind. *Out of your control, Jon.*

"But not yet," said Shaw. "Not yet. And as long as I breathe, I will do what I can to pull us back from the brink. To do what our world's governments have been unwilling, or unable to do. To implement real change. To save us, quite frankly."

"That's why I'm here," said Jon.

"I'm glad we're on the same page," said Shaw. "Because I see so much potential in your work, Jon. I know you must suspect that I brought you here for personal reasons."

Jon's eyes went back to Shaw's metal arm, his fingers still moving.

"The thought has come up," said Jon.

"I won't lie to you," said Shaw. "I want my arm back. But I imagine your son's disability has driven you and your research. Is that correct?"

"Yes," said Jon, images of shattered glass and broken metal floating through his head. He pushed them away, blinking.

"And I don't think that's a bad thing," said Shaw. "Extra fuel, extra motivation, is what separates the good from the great."

Jon thought to the sleepless nights, the long hours at the lab. He met Shaw's eyes.

"I want my arm back, Jon," said Shaw. "Just like you want Tommy's legs back. But I see so much more than that. Imagine a world where there are no lasting injuries. Imagine a world where we regrow limbs, heal bullet wounds. A world where injured organs regenerate. We can conquer trauma."

"That sounds great, Mr. Shaw, but in return, I don't want to lie to you," said Jon. "I don't know if we have the time for it. I've worked for years, and I've just gotten to the point where I can begin testing. It could be a long time before I get any real results, especially in humans."

Shaw shook his head then, emphatically. "I reject that."

"There are limits—"

"Not here, Jon," said Shaw. "Not here. You are not alone. A lot of people we've brought here have had trouble shaking these preconceptions about their work, about their research. They've been taught their whole lives, been educated about reasonable limits of science. About hypothesis, and tests. About the time needed to find good results. And I reject it."

"Good science takes time," said Jon.

"We don't have time, Jon," said Shaw. "But what we do have is resources. Infinite resources and cutting-edge technology. You will see once you get to your lab. But I want you to change your mindset, Jon. Think outside the box.

Don't worry about conserving resources. Think aggressively. Maybe even a little *recklessly*. There are no committees down here, and no politicians telling you how to do your research."

"I'll try my best," said Jon.

"That's all I ask," said Shaw. "Do you have any questions for me?"

"I have a lot of them, but most of them are simple things, like how do I do my laundry," said Jon.

"Operations is almost always the answer," said Shaw. "I want you focused on your work, not on chores."

"Then—can I talk to my ex-wife?" asked Jon. "Can I tell her we're safe?"

Shaw paused and looked at him, pondering an answer.

"That's a harder question," said Shaw.

"Sabrina said it's up to you," said Jon.

"She's not wrong," said Shaw. "The buck stops here, so to speak. We keep a strong grip on transmission to the outside. I'm worried about leaks. I'm concerned about our research being used for ill. I know that we have moles down here with us, spies. And controlling the means of communication is one of my weapons against them. I trust you, Jon, because like I said, your research is driven by personal reasons. But others, they can't be trusted so easily. You can write letters to her, Jon, to anyone, and they will be sent. Know that they will be read before that, but the only reason they would be denied is leaking information. As for calls, or video—that's impossible at this point. It leaves too much room for error."

"I just want her to know Tommy is safe," said Jon.

"I will make sure she knows," said Shaw. "Most have stronger feelings about their privacy."

"I just want to work," said Jon. "And none of your requirements seem that outlandish."

"Another reason to trust you," said Shaw, smiling again. "You recognize the need for some control. Any other questions?"

"I don't think so," said Jon. "Not right now. I'm sure I'll have more."

"I can't say that I'll always be available. I don't meet with everyone privately, but I wanted to talk to you in person. And if you'd like to speak again, I'll try and find the time."

"I appreciate that," said Jon. "I can't imagine how busy you are."

"It keeps me alive," said Shaw. "Before you go, I want to challenge you, Jon. I want you in the special projects lab. I want you there, but this is a meritocracy. You have to earn it. But I believe in you. I believe in your work. If it succeeds, if *you* succeed, it will become a part of my plan."

"Again, I'll do my best," said Jon.

"Do whatever is necessary," said Shaw. The fingers of his metal arm flexed back and forth. "This arm is rope. It's an incredible technology. In some ways, better than my actual arm ever was. It's strong, flexible, and incredibly responsive. But in the end, it's rope. It's not flesh." Shaw held it up.

"The next time I leave this lab, I will have my right arm again," said Shaw. "And your boy Tommy will walk alongside me, on his own two legs."

4

When Jon returned, Tommy was playing video games on the big screen in the living room. He wanted to check in with him, but he thought it best to give Tommy some time to adjust before they talked about anything. He was also just tired himself, after the long flight, and seeing a new place for the first time.

Their luggage was already waiting for them, and he unpacked his clothes, putting them away, and reading up on policies and FAQs, all present on his new tablet, locked to the Shawnet. It answered most of his questions, at least the ones that related to living his day-to-day life.

It didn't have answers about how to reconnect with his son after pulling away from his mother at her behest.

It didn't have answers about how to live in a panopticon.

It didn't have answers about how to make his research work on real life humans.

He looked out at Tommy, playing a game, sitting in their new living room. Jon wanted to go out there and talk to him, and ask him about his fears, and tell him about his, and his feet moved toward him, to sit down next to him. But then his heart was seized by a terror, a great abounding fear that he couldn't name or grasp, but was there, one he had forgotten in his absence.

He wanted to open up with his son, but the thought debilitated him. It exhausted him, just the thought of it. His time apart from Tommy and Maya had erased the heft of the emotional labor, of the simple act of caring so deeply. Of being around Tommy, his boy he loved so much and had injured so fundamentally. The constant reminder of an act he had worked at erasing since the night it happened.

Jon took a step back instead and went into the kitchen, and made them dinner. Sabrina hadn't lied. The kitchen had everything. Jon was a decent cook, but he only wanted simple, hearty food right now, so he cooked some chicken strips and mac n' cheese, straight from the box. It wasn't quite dinner time yet, but he was exhausted, and hungry.

He cooked as Tommy played, and soon food was ready. He brought Tommy a plate, and then ate as he watched Tommy play, a first-person shooter that Jon couldn't recognize. He ate quietly, and Tommy offered no words, focusing on his game.

"If that's not enough, there's more in the fridge. I'm going to relax in my room. Let me know if you need anything. Okay?"

Tommy only nodded, never looking over at Jon, half a

relief and half a burden.

Jon retreated to his bedroom and realized looking through his computer that all his research had already been scanned and cataloged. He read through it until his exhaustion overtook him. He laid down in bed and went to sleep.

*

"Nice to meet you, Dr. Matthews. I'm excited to work with you. Your research sure is fascinating. I studied all of it last night. I think I understand most of it, but how do you plan on matching the rate of caloric absorption with the rate of regeneration? It seems like that's the chokepoint for rapid reconstruction, and human bodies can only absorb—"

Mel Underwood spoke quickly, her black ponytail bobbing behind her with every word. Jon had come down to see his lab, now ready for him, but before he could take a breath, he met his new assistant, who clearly had more energy than him.

"Mel?" he asked, finally interrupting her.

"Yes, Doctor?" she asked.

"Could you slow down, for just a moment?" asked Jon. "I'm still waking up. And you can call me Jon."

Mel stood just shorter than Jon, waifish to the point Jon worried a stiff wind would blow her away. Her lab coat enveloped her.

She smiled skittishly. "Sorry. I've been chomping at the bit to get to work."

"I understand," said Jon. He had left Tommy at the facility's school, where all the staff's children were sorted into groups and taught. Tommy hadn't been happy, hadn't seen the need for it, but Jon wouldn't hear dissent.

After a cup of coffee, he felt human again, and Mel's

words finally sounded like speech. Mel had come in later in the day yesterday, after Jon himself, but had not been affected by the same level of exhaustion Jon had. Maybe it was because she hadn't met Eaton Shaw face to face. Or maybe it was because her energy was indefatigable.

When he returned with his coffee, Mel had pulled up his notes on a large screen on the wall.

"God," said Jon. "I've never seen my work so big."

"I hope it's okay," said Mel. "I've kinda started organizing the place already." Jon looked around at his lab for the first time. It was impressive. Stainless steel lab tables, multiple computer workstations, and screens everywhere. Whiteboards lined one wall, with various empty workspaces that they could change however they wanted.

"It looks fine," said Jon. "This is our space. We can do what we want with it."

"Well, what do we want to do?" asked Mel.

"You said you read through all my research? All my notes?" asked Jon.

"Everything they had on the computer," said Mel.

"Well, there's not much more than that. I broke into the lab after they shut it down to get the last scraps. I'm sure there's a few things stored on the cloud somewhere that we're missing, but nothing important."

"Where do we start?" asked Mel. "It seems like you have the fundamental science down, but you never got to test."

"No," said Jon. "Never had the means or the permission for it."

"I don't think we need approval for anything, here," said Mel.

"No," said Jon. "Shaw told me himself he wants results

within a year. Faster if possible. Which seems impossible. It took me years just to get to this point, where I have the procedure theoretically working, but never in practice. I'm sure we can get rats here, but testing them will take forever. Even if we're testing multiple in a day, waiting for efficacy results will take weeks, if not months, and that's just rats—"

"What if we use simulations to test for us and use the most probable successful formulas from it?"

"Well, that'd be great," said Jon. "But we would need model rat genomes, plus the power to compute an ungodly amount of calculations. Hell, just for *one* rat, for *one* procedure—I can't imagine the number of variables—"

"They have it," said Mel. "I've looked through the resources, and this place has enough capacity to run thousands at a time. More than we could ever use, honestly. I mean, there are hundreds of labs, so it would have to."

"It has the genomes as well?" asked Jon.

"Yes, everything," said Mel. "Basically every animal."

"We'd still have to model the serum, and caloric absorption rates, and regeneration—"

"I can do that," said Mel.

"What?" asked Jon. "You can?"

"Well, yeah," said Mel. "It's my focus, my specialty. I imagine it's why I was assigned to you." Jon hadn't thought of Mel's qualifications. He'd just assumed she was a biologist, like him. But Shaw had recruited her with intention. Everything had a purpose down here, even if it didn't seem like it at first. "Half the work is done already, frankly. It might take me a few days to finish it, and should be good enough to start then. I can finesse any problems as we work."

"Well, holy hell," said Jon. "Get started. Let me know if

you have any issues, but otherwise, full steam ahead. I have a meeting with Baskins in a few minutes, and I'll get the rest of the equipment we need."

Mel got to work, sitting at a workstation she had claimed for herself, three screens in front of her. She typed rapidly, lines of code filling up the screen.

Jon didn't extend a hand for a handshake when he went into Baskin's office. Donald shut the doors behind him, and the glass frosted over around them.

"Everything looking good in your lab?" asked Donald.

"I mean, I just moved in, but yeah, it looks like it will suit our needs."

"Is Dr. Underwood adequate as an assistant?" asked Donald.

"Again, I just met her, but she seems brilliant," said Jon. "Almost intimidatingly so."

"Good," said Donald, smiling behind his desk. "Mr. Shaw earmarked her for you."

"That makes sense," said Jon. "She seems perfect."

"Well, that aside," said Donald. "I've read through your work, and I understand the basics, but could you lay out what a clear plan of progress for your lab looks like?"

"Well," said Jon. "Mel is currently building computer models to test possible serums. It will allow us to spend time on only the most promising formulas and not waste time on the dregs. She said that would take a few days. In the meantime, I would organize the lab, and lay out—"

Donald waved him off. "I don't need the play-by-play. Just the big picture. The macro. What does success look like and how will you get there?"

"I mean, success is full regeneration of a human limb.

How to get there? That's more complicated. Finding the right serum is the first step."

"What will the right serum do?" asked Donald.

"There's a lot of jargon—I don't know how comfortable—"

"Give me the layman's version."

"It will do three things. One—it will convert the cells at the wound site into what basically amount to stem cells. Cells that can be used in the healing process to recreate all the different types of tissue needed. The bone, the muscle, the skin, the everything. Two—it will accelerate the healing process into hyperdrive. Even if we could get the healing process to work, it would take a long time to finish, especially in humans. Years, possibly. Even in ideal situations, no human can be confined for that long. So we have to speed that up."

"How fast can you make it?" asked Donald. He was writing notes in a notepad. He scribbled quickly.

"I mean, the limit is only the constraints of the body, and that brings me to the third thing it would need to do, which I haven't figured out yet."

"And that is?"

"The third would be to accelerate the rate of caloric absorption. You can't create something from nothing. There has to be fuel. And however much I combine oral and intravenous injection, it's not fast enough. I can get results in rats quickly enough, but it will be a problem when I scale up to larger animals, who have more complicated systems and are just—bigger."

"So, if I understand it, the problem is we can't eat and absorb calories quick enough to provide the rate of healing we want?"

"Yes, basically," said Jon. "And I don't have a solution for it. Even if an animal is eating food that is incredibly calorically dense, it can't convert those cells fast enough. It's a two-fold problem, and what I'll be trying to solve while Mel is modeling."

"Okay," said Donald. "I'm going to look into it, and see if any of our other projects can help you with that. But let's say we solve that issue. What then?"

"Once that's solved, it's about finding the right serum, testing it on a live rat, and then, if that succeeds, moving onto larger animals, in graduated steps, until we finally get to humans. But on Mr. Shaw's timescale, even with the computer modeling, I just don't see how it's possible to move fast enough."

"We'll play it by ear," said Donald. "You tell me what you require, and we'll get moving. I'll make sure there won't be any delays on your resources."

"Well, I need rats. I have almost everything else I need in the lab already. It's a pretty comprehensive kit in there."

"We have thousands of rats," said Donald. "And basically any other animal. How many do you want?"

"Ten to start," said Jon. "We'll need more."

"I'll connect you with our quartermaster," said Donald. "You hit a button, he'll get more up here."

"Thanks," said Jon.

"Let me know if you need anything else, and I mean literally anything. And keep me updated with any progress."

"Will do," said Jon. Donald stood up and opened the doors, the glass defrosting.

"That was a fast meeting," said Jon.

"Words are cheap," said Donald.

"I'm going to get to work," said Jon, and he left Donald's office, heading back to his lab, less than a hundred feet away. He turned around a frosted glass corner and ran smack dab into someone. Jon fell in a shower of papers, dazed. He looked up to see the big man from the day before, the one who glared at him. His eyes looked similarly now, as he stared down at Jon and his empty hands.

"Sorry," said Jon. "I didn't—"

"Didn't look where you were going?" asked the man.

"I guess not," said Jon, even though he couldn't have helped it if he had tried.

"You should be more careful, Dr. Matthews," said the man.

"You have me at a disadvantage," said Jon, waiting for him to extend a hand to help him up. It didn't come, and Jon pushed himself off the floor.

"Dr. Stone," said the man. Jon picked up the papers for him. Stone didn't help him.

"Nice to meet you," said Jon.

Stone didn't answer, only glared at him.

Jon slowly stopped picking up the papers, handing Stone the few he had grabbed. This was more than just Jon running into him.

"Do we have a problem? Did I do something wrong?" asked Jon.

Dr. Stone held his glare. He shook his head, sighing. He narrowed his eyes.

"Your lab is twice the size of mine," said Stone.

"I'm—I'm sorry," said Jon. "I'm sure—"

"And they gave you Dr. Underwood," said Stone, cutting

him off. Jon didn't bother speaking again. "Limb regeneration, right?"

"Yes," said Jon, finally.

"You've been on the surface more recently than I have," said Stone. "Maybe you can tell me. Is there a huge rash of missing limbs killing thousands of people?"

Jon stared back at him, at Stone's dark, unblinking eyes.

"Oh, there isn't?" asked Stone. "Not a terrible emergency, you say?"

"I was invited down here—"

"You were invited down here because Shaw wants his arm back. Period. End of story. Close book. Anything else he tells you is a lie." Stone got closer to him, peering down at him. He stood six inches taller than Jon, his shoulders broad. Jon didn't budge.

"*Do* we have a problem, Doctor?" asked Stone. "Yes. It's you. *You're* the problem. You're taking up space and attention from other projects. Everyone else is here to save the world. You're here to regrow a billionaire's arm."

Stone turned and left. His assistant came out a moment later and picked up the fallen papers.

Jon stood there, taking deep breaths. He wouldn't let his anger guide him. He breathed out until he was calm, and then he returned to his lab.

"Are you okay?" asked Mel.

"I'm okay," said Jon. "Why do you ask?"

"Dr. Stone looked like he was about to crush you," said Mel.

Jon paused. "He doesn't appreciate my presence here," said Jon.

"He seems like a dick," said Mel.

Jon didn't answer, and Mel returned to her work. Jon began brainstorming ideas and tried to push Stone's comments out of his mind.

Mel wasn't wrong. Stone was assuredly an asshole.

But Jon was worried that he also might be right.

5

The cafeteria was a gigantic space, with rows of tables lined up, hundreds of seats, all given ample room to spread out and eat.

But the place was mostly empty. A lone eater got up just as Jon entered, putting his tray back and throwing away his trash.

It felt eerie, but Jon's stomach wouldn't wait, so he went up to the old-fashioned cafeteria line and grabbed a little bit of everything. To be honest, he was starving, and he tried to thank all the lunchroom workers. He wondered where they came from. Were they Shaw's employees up top? Did they get to bring their families?

Jon took his tray of food and cup of water and sat down in the middle of a long table. His chair scraped against the floor. It echoed throughout the room. He ate slowly, enjoying the food. It was great, much better than typical cafeteria fare. Shaw had spared no expense. Jon stared idly as he ate. A few people came through, all grabbing something to go.

He looked down to his food, Stone's comments ringing back through his head. Stone had accused him of just being here to regrow Shaw's arm.

But was it true? Why *was* he here?

Everything had happened so quickly, he hadn't really thought of the why. The richest man on Earth had thrown him a hail mary, a way to continue his research and keep his son safe, all at the same time. Why would he have said no? Out of some misbegotten drive to give resources only to those who had completely altruistic reasons?

Jon had never bought into that. If anyone did good, it didn't matter why they did it. If it was to earn respect, or credibility, or if it was only out of the goodness of their heart, it still brought good into the world. Good done for selfish reasons was still good.

Of course, I would think that. I wouldn't be doing this if not for Tommy.

After the accident, he had pivoted his research. How could he not? And of course it was part of the reason he worked at it. Shaw mentioned it himself. The drive, the personal reasons that fed his study and his work.

Jon didn't know Stone's reasons for coming down here, or even what his research was, but Jon didn't need to know. He didn't need to prove to him, or to anyone the value of his research. This wasn't a zero-sum game. Shaw had all the resources in the world to spread around. Sure, the environment was competitive, but that was no different than up on the surface.

I just have to keep my head down and do the work. Stone doesn't—

"Is this seat free?" asked a female voice. He looked up to see the face and curly hair of the doctor from the Energy lab, who's eyes he had caught for half a second.

"Sorry. Taken," he said, straightfaced. She only stared at him, and then he broke, smiling. "Joking. Please, sit."

She smiled, and it lit up her face, a slight gap between her two front teeth. "You almost had me." She sat down, putting her food down in front of her.

"I'm Jon," he said.

"I know," she said, still smiling.

"You do?" asked Jon.

"Of course," she said. "You're going to give our fearless leader his arm back."

"Oh, Jesus Christ," said Jon. "Word gets around quickly, doesn't it?"

"It's no different down here than it was up there," she said. "I'm Tabby. Tabby Knight."

"Nice to meet you," he said. "Is it always this empty in here?"

"Yes," said Tabby. "Most people get their lunch delivered and eat at their desk. Or standing, or wherever. I'm just one of those weirdos who likes taking a break for lunch. And I guess you are too."

"Yeah, I suppose so," said Jon.

"Work isn't everything," said Tabby.

"Well, I'm still a terrible workaholic," said Jon. "But I'll take my small victories over my worst habits, and stealing a lunch for myself every day is one of them. Even before the world started falling apart. I always took a lunch away from my desk."

"How productive are you when you're eating, anyway?"

"Not very," said Jon. "And there's less crumbs."

"That's how you get ants," said Tabby.

Jon laughed. "I don't think that's much of a concern down here."

"No, probably not," said Tabby. "But you never know. They get into the damnedest places."

"So, you're in Energy, right?" asked Jon. "Am I allowed to ask what you're working on? Or is that classified?"

"Everyone's projects are in the computer, if you dig a little," said Tabby. "Unless you're in the special projects lab. But I don't know if anyone's there yet. Unless Shaw seeded it before I got here. Which is certainly possible."

"Then here. What are you working on?" asked Jon.

"Batteries," said Tabby.

"Batteries?" asked Jon. "Is that it?"

"Yeah," said Tabby. "Batteries."

"I assume they're super special batteries," said Jon.

"Well, yes," said Tabby. "They're incredibly small, incredibly dense batteries, while still being lightweight. They can carry enough energy to power a town for a week in what amounts to a light backpack. Or, they will, once we get them working."

"I would categorize them as special," said Jon. "That seems almost miraculous."

"It'll change everything," said Tabby. "It will change how our infrastructure works, especially once we make them cheap. Even better, they don't use any rare earth metals, so we'll be able to make a lot of them."

"Wow," said Jon.

"Eh," said Tabby. She took a bite of pizza.

"Eh?" asked Jon.

"Eh," she said. "Something about counting eggs in baskets."

"Sounds like you're close," said Jon.

"I've been close before," said Tabby. "And it didn't amount to anything."

"Fair enough," said Jon. "I feel like I've never been 'close.'"

"Well, you're researching limb regeneration, right?" asked Tabby. "That's science fiction. That's The Lizard from Spider-Man."

"So was space travel, once upon a time," said Jon. "And then we tackled it. Shaw told me to think outside the box, but I feel like I've been doing that my whole career."

"You've met him?" asked Tabby.

"Yeah, yesterday, after I got in," said Jon.

"Faaaancy," said Tabby. "All of us rabble only get to see him at the facility wide pep talks."

"I guess I am special, then," said Jon.

"If I was a billionaire, and I lost an arm, I'd probably try and get it back if I could," said Tabby. "It's his money, his lab. No shame in it."

"Well, there is when everyone else is trying to save the world," said Jon.

Tabby shrugged. "Eh," she said. "Will it help people?"

"Yes," said Jon. "If we can get it to work reliably."

"Then what's the problem?" asked Tabby.

"I guess there isn't one," said Jon. "Except for Dr. Stone, who doesn't seem to like me."

"That happens," said Tabby. She took another bite of pizza. "Fuck him."

Jon laughed loudly. Tabby smiled and shrugged. "He'll deal. He should worry about his research."

"I haven't looked at what it is," said Jon.

"Big guy, right?" asked Tabby.

"Yeah," said Jon. "Do you know what it is?"

"No," said Tabby. "But I've seen him around. And I'm sure he's working on something valuable. He wouldn't be down here if he wasn't. Shaw hasn't brought anyone down who isn't. We're all brilliant. We're all special. It's one of the reasons I came down here."

"Not to save the world?"

"I mean, that's part of it," said Tabby. "It's not like I was doing anything productive up top. Sitting in my underwear and eating cheerios, hoping someone else would be able to save the world. Down here, I'm working. And there's not much up there for me, anyway. Folks died when I was just out of college. No kids, no spouse. A couple friends, but I wasn't seeing them. Might as well do some good, and work with the smartest people on the planet."

Jon stared at her. *Wow.*

"Something on my face?" asked Tabby.

"No," said Jon, smiling. "Sorry."

"It's okay," she said, and smiled back. "So, what was he like?"

"Who?" asked Jon.

"Shaw," said Tabby. "What was he like, just you and him?"

"Very smart," said Jon. "It's like that thing, where you meet someone who you know is going to be a salesman to you. They're going to have a big personality and try and convince you of something. And you know that, going in, so you have your guard up. Do you get me?"

"I think so," said Tabby. "Like buying a car."

"Exactly," said Jon. "But most of the time, my guard stays up. I keep them out. Not Shaw. I couldn't. Either he's the best salesman I've ever met, or he honestly believes in this place. Believes in me. It kinda felt like I was talking to my dad."

"He's very good at it," said Tabby. "And he's absolutely invested in this place. But I would keep your distance. Keep your head and your heart your own."

"Why do you say that?" asked Jon.

"I don't trust him," said Tabby.

"No?" asked Jon.

"No. As a matter of course," said Tabby. "He's a billionaire. His problems are entirely disconnected from ours. He might as well be an alien. Sure, he's invested a lot of cash in this place. More than you or I will ever see in our entire lives. And he definitely wants the world to work again, because he needs it to make him money, and he wants to leave his house without walking into a riot, just like anyone else—but he's not like us, and don't forget it for a second. And don't forget about the power of this science we're developing after everything is fixed."

"Isn't everything down here fairly useful to everyone?" asked Jon. "It doesn't seem like capitalism is driving this."

Tabby shrugged. "It's hard to say. What if they're used for evil, after everything is cleaned up? What if *Shaw* uses them for evil after everything is cleaned up?"

"I mean, it's a possibility," said Jon. "But there's always a chance of that, on whatever we work on."

"Only difference is down here, we can't just quit," said Tabby. "I'm not in a hurry to go back to the surface, and if I have a difference of opinion about how to use my batteries, I don't have much of a choice in the matter. Shaw has the power down here. He controls everything."

"But you still came," said Jon.

"I did," said Tabby. "Because sometimes you have to take a chance. Sometimes hope is the only option. So I hope that after I make my batteries, they're not abused by dictators, or sold for a premium to only the super rich."

"I should get back to work," said Jon.

"So should I," said Tabby. "Same time tomorrow?"

"That sounds great," said Jon. Tabby stood up and Jon tried not to stare too hard at her as she walked away. She didn't look back.

Jon returned to his lab, with Mel still working.

He tried to focus on his work, but his mind kept returning to Tabby.

6

"How was your day at school?" asked Jon.

He was cooking dinner for them again, this time something a little more involved than mac n' cheese. He was trying to make blackened grouper, with a side of wild rice, with a garlic sauce for the fish. The blackening season wasn't working for some reason.

Tommy played the same game in the living room while Jon cooked. Jon had greeted him when he got back to their new home, but Tommy hadn't said a word. Jon felt something in the house with them. A coldness. He hoped dinner would dispel it, but no luck so far.

He finished cooking and plated everything, putting it on their small dining set adjacent to the living room.

"Tommy," said Jon. "Come eat at the table."

"I'm playing," said Tommy.

"You can play again after we're finished," said Jon. "I promise. Pause it and come eat. You need to eat, anyway." Jon waited, listening, and then heard the sound of gunfire from the game stop, and Tommy wheeled over to the table, a chair removed so he could sit.

"What'd you make?" asked Tommy.

"Grouper and rice," said Jon. "Hope that's okay."

"It's fine," said Tommy. He cut into the fish and ate a bite. Jon ate with him, glancing at him. Tommy didn't look up once.

"How was your first real day?" asked Jon.

"It was fine," said Tommy.

"Did you meet any other kids?" asked Jon.

"A couple of them," said Tommy. "But we didn't have much time to talk."

"Well, maybe you'll be able to get to know them. To make friends."

"Maybe," said Tommy, still not looking up.

"Did you have a teacher?" asked Jon.

"A few different ones," said Tommy. "Depending on the subject. They rotated us around. The different age groups."

"What did you learn?" asked Jon.

"I don't know," said Tommy. "I mostly just got homework."

"Have you done it yet?"

"Not yet."

"When are you going to do it?"

"Later," said Tommy.

Tommy still hadn't looked at him.

"Tommy," said Jon. "Tommy. Look at me."

Tommy looked up from his food after a moment, his eyebrows arcing up in a question.

"Yes?" asked Tommy.

"What is up with you? Are you okay?"

Tommy pursed his lips and looked away. He took a deep breath.

"Why are we here, Dad?" he asked, finally.

"What do you mean? You know why we're here. I'm working on my research. You're safe here."

"But Mom's not here," said Tommy.

"She wanted to help people, and she can't do that down here," said Jon. "But she wanted you to be safe."

"I want to be with her," said Tommy.

"We had an opportunity, and we took it," said Jon. "We can't see your mom right now."

"One of the other kids said they hadn't talked to their dad in three months," said Tommy. "And hasn't heard anything from him at all. No messages, no nothing."

"We can send her letters," said Jon.

"I don't want to send her a letter," said Tommy. "I want to talk to her face to face. I want to make sure she's alright. We left her alone up there!"

Jon took a deep breath. "She chose to stay up there, Tommy. And she wanted for you to come down here. She wants you safe, and there's nowhere safer than here."

"Yeah, because we're a thousand miles from nowhere! We don't even know where we are. Somewhere in Canada, probably."

"How do you know that?" asked Jon.

"It was cold when we got outside the plane," said Tommy. "And it took us five hours to fly, and I looked up the specs on that jet. I'm guessing we're in northern Canada. But we don't know where. We're trapped here."

"We would be trapped anywhere we were," said Jon. "We don't have to think about riots here, or martial law."

"No, we only have to worry about cameras watching us every second."

Jon sighed.

"It's better than the alternative, Tommy. I know it's hard on you, being so far away from everything you know, but you have to be patient. The work being done down here is what's going to right the ship up top. I'm just doing my part."

"You're not here to help anyone." Tommy still stared down at his food, and Jon's heart turned cold at his words.

"What?"

"You're not here to help anyone. You're here because you want to fix me."

"That's—"

"That's all you've ever wanted. And now you have your perfect chance."

"Tommy—"

"Tell me it's not the reason," said Tommy, staring at him now. Jon stared back and then looked away. He couldn't say it. He couldn't lie to Tommy.

"That's what I thought," said Tommy. "I don't blame you for what happened. How many times do I have to say it? I'm not broken, Dad. It's not your fault."

Tommy held his stare for a second longer, and then reversed, and pushed himself to his room without a glance back.

Jon's heart burned cold, and he took another deep breath. He wanted to storm after Tommy, and yell at him about everything that had led to this moment, but it wouldn't do any good. Because Tommy was right. The root of it all was him.

Jon finished his food and put away the rest of it. He turned off Tommy's video game and the television, and went to his room. He pulled open the drawers in the corner desk until he found a stack of paper with a FUTURE lab letterhead.

Maya,

I don't know when you'll get this. They say we can send letters, but no calls or video. First, we're here. We're safe. I don't know where here is, but it's secure and protected.

I have my own lab, with an assistant, and an incredible amount of resources. I met Eaton Shaw, which apparently isn't the norm for everyone here. He's very charismatic, and very smart. He knows what he wants. And I'm going to try and help. I don't know if my work will actually be that helpful. Shaw seems to think so. I'm not so sure.

Tommy is angry at me. He doesn't want to be here, and I don't fault him. And he misses you, and I don't blame him for that either. But I think we made the right decision, regardless of everything else. He's safer here than back home.

He said that I'm just trying to fix him. And really, that's the root of all of it, isn't it? It's the problem I can't research away. And I know I ended up failing us because of it.

Jon stopped and erased the last paragraph.

I'm going to do my best to help, to get us back with solutions to all the problems. Everyone down here is working as hard as they can to make sure we fix things.

There's no way for you to reply to this, but know that we're safe. Take care of yourself. Be careful. I know it's not in you to give up, which is why you stayed behind. Tommy will learn that.

I'll send another letter soon.

-Jon

Jon folded it up and put it in an envelope, addressing it. He didn't know what to do with it, though. It's not like they had a post office. He picked up the phone and called Operations. A stern voiced man answered and told him there would be someone there to grab it in ten minutes.

They came within a minute, and Jon handed it off, hoping it would get where it needed to.

Talk to Tommy.

He took a deep breath and followed the instructions his heart gave him. Jon went to Tommy's door and knocked. There was no answer.

"Tommy?" he asked at the door.

"What?" asked Tommy.

"I'm—I'm—are you okay?" asked Jon.

"I'm fine," said Tommy.

"Are you sure?"

"I'm sure," said Tommy.

Jon's hand closed around the knob, going to turn it, to go in there and apologize to his son, apologize for everything, for trying so hard for so long and making it all worse in the process, but he couldn't do it. It was too deep inside him, too intertwined in him. It was *him* now, and he couldn't cut the string. He would unravel.

So Jon retreated.

He went to his room, where he dove into the Shawnet database, into the different research projects. He looked at Tabby's first, out of sheer curiosity. And as far as he could tell, she was true to her word, even though he didn't understand most of the jargon in the summary for her project. He couldn't figure out most of the vocabulary in most of the capsules, but they still fascinated him. Half of them seemed impossible, like science fiction. Did Shaw expect them all to succeed? Fusion at room temperature. Weather control. All of these things felt silly.

But then he thought to his own work, and the disbelief he often confronted when he told people his goals.

There was some solace in that. Jon belonged here, in the simple fact that he was trying to do the impossible.

7

The days passed in a blur. Jon settled into a silent truce with Tommy, and he continued to see Tabby at lunches. He liked her, and he wanted to ask her out, but he didn't know what that entailed down here, so he just tried to enjoy her company during the short time when he wasn't working.

Because what he mostly did was work. Mel had coded his formula and built a model to test it on the rat genome on file. It toiled away, testing efficacy after efficacy of thousand permutations of serums, some giant server somewhere spinning up rack after rack of computer power.

"How are we doing?" asked Jon.

"We've gotten a few viable options," said Mel. "We'll get more as we go, and any actual testing we'll do I can add to the model, to dial in the accuracy."

The rats sat in a corner in a couple of cages, eating, sleeping, doing their normal rat business. Mel went over and stared at them.

"Splinter isn't eating today," said Mel.

"You shouldn't name them," said Jon. "It's going to make it harder when we have to test on them."

"I know," said Mel. "But I can't help it. I've never liked it."

"What, testing on animals?" asked Jon.

"Yeah," said Mel. "I don't even eat meat, and now we're going to chop up these little guys. And I know there's even more of them throughout this lab in particular. Poor little ratties."

"I mean, it's not nice, I know," said Jon. "But it's necessary. It bothered me at first, but then—"

"You got used to it," said Mel. "I know, that's what everyone says. But I never got used to it."

"You kill enough rats," said Jon, "and you get used to it."

"I don't want to become used to it," said Mel. "Killing defenseless animals."

"They don't suffer," said Jon. "And it's not like we're testing cosmetics. We're experimenting so we can help people. Save lives, in some cases. And like it or not, that wouldn't happen without these little guys. Frankly, your models are saving a lot of them."

"I know," said Mel. "But it's still hard."

"Well, I'm going to prep a serum," said Jon. "So get one ready."

"We're moving ahead?" asked Mel.

"No time like the present," said Jon. "We've got to get going, if we want to find results."

Mel thought for a moment and then grabbed a rat, carrying it over to their experimentation area. Jon went to his workstation and pulled the most promising serum from Mel's model, letting the computer give the Cas9 enzymes the proper instructions using CRISPR, and then attaching them to a virus that would insert it at the right spot.

CRISPR made this all possible, and gene editing was where Jon had gotten his start. After the accident, he pivoted when he realized what the system could do with the appropriate research. So much advancement had been made over the years, eliminating toxicity and other complications. But it was still hard. Harder still when you were trying to do new things with it. Mammals regenerating limbs was still new, and he was the only one attempting it. This was all him.

Even so, the computer modeling made it much, much faster, weeding out any toxic combinations quickly. But it didn't mean this was foolproof. The DNA cuts could still destroy the animal, or the replacement DNA or RNA could be wrong in a million different ways. The cells could proliferate, cause cancers, or obliterate any number of perfectly functional systems within the animal. It was messy. Jon hated it, but if they would ever get anywhere, they'd have to start here.

The computer also mixed the resultant serum, so Jon didn't have to do it by hand, which was how he trained. He hadn't realized how much time that would save him. It would take him a day to put together a mixture manually, examine it, and then test it. The computer did it in five minutes. Jon had heard about these systems, but he thought they were only prototypes at this point. Shaw had dozens of them on this level alone.

Mel had grabbed a rat, and Jon didn't ask its name. He

washed up and put on gloves and a mask. Mel sedated the rat, sliding a small IV into it. It would keep it under, both to prevent it from unnecessary pain, and from keeping it from moving. The IV would carry sedatives and nutrients, feeding the rat as many extra calories as its tiny body could handle.

"You ready?" asked Jon.

"Ready and recording," said Mel. They would record every experiment for archival and research purposes.

"Okay," said Jon, breathing deeply. His heart beat hard in his chest. He had thought a lot about this moment, but excitement had never entered his mind, but he was excited now. This was was as far as he had ever gotten..

They had reached the edge of the map. *Here there be dragons.*

He took a scalpel and held it, squeezing it hard. *Now for the tough part.* He laid out the rat's right arm, and sliced through it, near its shoulder. The scalpel was sharp, and it cut the flesh easily. Blood spurted from the rat, and Mel took gauze and held it tight to the wound. Meanwhile, Jon grabbed heavy shears, and with a SNAP, cut through the bone quickly. Mel held the gauze there, staunching the flow of blood.

If they did nothing, the rat would bleed to death. But Jon moved quickly, and grabbed the syringe, the syringe that held the key to everything. It would insert a payload within a payload within a payload, all supercharged, engineered to deliver a specific enzyme as rapidly as possible, rearranging the rat's genetic code, changing parts of it so that instead of trying to stop the bleeding, and create scar tissue, it would prioritize regrowing the limb. Directions to change flesh at the wound site into stem cells, so they can be re-purposed to regrow bone, and muscle, and flesh.

Jon slid the syringe into the rat and injected the material. It wasn't a lot. It didn't need to be. CRISPR technology had advanced a lot since its inception, and Shaw had pushed it even further. Changes to the genome could take days or weeks before. Now it was minutes. Shaw hadn't been kidding when he said he wanted change quickly.

And within minutes, the regrowth had started. Blood loss had slowed, and then stopped, and the arm regrew in front of their eyes. The IV drip was nutrient rich, trying to give the rat as much fuel as they could, to burn for the pyre that was churning near its severed arm.

But it was still slow. Incremental. Within a few minutes, the regeneration slowed even further.

"We've burnt through all its reserve," said Jon. "At least the safeguards are working. It's not stealing from the muscle tissue in the rest of the animal. Now it can only heal as quickly as we deliver the nutrients through the IV."

"How long will it take?" asked Mel.

"I don't know," said Jon. "Probably hours, at this rate. We can start a few others, with different serum models and other delivery methods for CRISPR. See if there's any change."

They worked hard, and in sequence, they repeated the procedure. Sedating a rat, amputating its arm, and then injecting a different serum into it, wondering if any of the results would be different, more or less effective, faster, slower, more efficient. They measured hundreds of variables, and soon all their space was filled with a half dozen rats, all sedated, all slowly regenerating limbs.

"A watched pot never boils," said Jon, as Mel stared at

them, her eyes glued to the different rats.

"I shouldn't have named them," said Mel.

"Every day is a learning experience," said Jon. "The next batch you'll know better."

"What do you mean, the next batch?" asked Mel. "What if one of these is a winner?"

"I appreciate your optimism," said Jon. "But I'm not holding my breath. In my experience, if you can glean anything positive to move forward with from the first set of tests, you've done well. But none of these will be a final serum, even for the rats."

Mel sighed and pressed her lips together.

"You should probably just do other work," said Jon. "We can check back throughout the day." Mel nodded, and went back to her workstation, and soon her mechanical keyboard clacked like a machine gun.

Jon tried to do the same, but found it hard to follow his own advice. He wanted to remain optimistic as well, that somehow with all the advanced Shaw tech, they would stumble onto a breakthrough right away. That the results, although slow, would work, and they could move onto a larger animal for the next round of testing. That Shaw's goals weren't ridiculous. That human results would be tangible in the near future.

Jon stole glances at the rats as the day wore on. After hours, he forced himself back to his station, to plan for the next day, and the next week. He let his mind wander, to Tommy, to Maya, to Tabby, still blankly staring at the screen, full of contingencies and possibilities to explore with the subsequent set of modeling.

Was Maya doing okay up top? She was the most dependable person he'd ever met, one of the mentally toughest, one of the reasons he had fallen in love with her. Her tenacity and willpower had impressed him more than anything. It was always something he had struggled with, and he had admired it in her.

She's doing fine. She's contributing. Hell, even if they shut the hospital down, she'd probably do triage work in her living room. But nothing could stop her.

"Jon!" said Mel, and her sudden voice broke him out of his thoughts. He looked to her. She must have been trying to get his attention.

"Sorry," he said. His eyes flitted to the clock on his screen. *Oh shit, results.* He had lost track of time. The rats would be finished regenerating by now.

"What do they look like?" asked Jon, only able to see Mel's face, not yet the rats. He thought her face told him all he needed to know. Failure. He had expected it to be fair, but he always hoped for success, even minimal success. He got up and walked over to see the results for himself.

Mel's expression hadn't prepared him.

He had expected half formed limbs, or the wrong number of fingers, or arms that didn't function at all. Unacceptable mutations, and certainly unpleasant to look at, but it was a spectrum of failure he had prepared himself for, especially in his field of research. Anyone who had studied biology had dissected numerous animals and seen lots of violence inflicted on them. And in his study, he'd seen hundreds if not thousands of pictures of amputees, of battle trauma, of victims of car accidents and construction mishaps. Ghastly things, that after enough exposure, had desensitized him to a certain extent. He didn't know how Mel worked, but he had assumed the rats would have some level of deformation.

He hadn't expected this. None of the six rats looked identical, but all of their regrown limbs had mutated. But they weren't half formed. If anything, they were *over*grown. The limbs had grown bulbous, red, inflating with muscle, and fat, and bone. Some had bone spikes poking through their skin, where they leaked blood. Others had sets of multiple paws, all in a row next to each other. One in particular had a limb cartoonishly long, twice as long as a normal limb, thick with disgusting muscle, impossible and distended. It twitched, and he felt a twinge in his gut, and he averted his eyes for a second, taking a deep breath.

But he looked back.

"What should we do?" asked Mel.

"Record results," he said. "On every animal, and then we euthanize them. I'll dissect them."

Mel looked at him, and then back at the animals, and then she broke, holding a hand over her mouth, and running to the trash can. She threw up, her hands holding the can tight to her face. She finished, spitting a few more times. She tentatively put it down and went to her desk, drinking from a bottle of water.

"I—I wasn't ready for—whatever this is," said Mel.

"You're doing a good job," said Jon. "But next time, be ready. Because we will see worse."

Mel nodded and retrieved her notebook and prepared the vials of euthanizing agent. It would kill them quickly and painlessly. Jon readied for dissection.

8

Jon knocked on the door, feeling halfway silly. Here he was, in Star Trek land, and he was knocking on doors. But he didn't know what else to do. He felt a pit in his stomach that no amount of deep breathing could banish.

It's just dinner, you dummy. You've eaten lunch with her dozens of times at this point.

But it wasn't just dinner. It was a date. And putting that label on it had made the easy context of a conversation over a meal feel like summiting Mt. Everest.

It had been a few weeks since the first experiment, and they had found little positive in their research in the intervening time. They had repeated experiments on dozens and dozens of rats, with various permutations of the serum, over and over again, but no matter which version they used, the rats came out wrong. The mutations and deformities continued. His work hours had stretched longer and longer. He still ate lunch with Tabby every day, and his admiration of her had grown into a full on crush.

Still, he didn't ask her out. He didn't know what was considered appropriate here. They were colleagues, but he had his hands full with his research, so he would let their friendship remain just that.

Until Tabby asked him over for dinner.

"Do you want to come over tonight?" she had asked. His heart jumped a little at the question. He almost choked on his sandwich. He had to force it down, taking a big swallow of water.

Tabby had to hold back laughter. "Are you okay?" she asked.

Jon nodded, the water helping. Tabby still smiled at him.

"Sorry," he said.

"It's okay," she said. "Well?"

"I—I would like to…"

"Buuuuutt…"

"And believe me, I think you're great…"

"Buuuuutt…"

"But I don't know if us—if we—if us seeing each outside of work is appropriate," he said, finally managing to get it out.

Tabby burst out laughing at that. He stared at her, feeling a little lost.

"What? What's so funny?"

"You really do only focus on your work, don't you?" she asked, after she had stopped laughing.

"I mean, I don't know," said Jon.

"Have you taken a look around at all? Noticed anything about your co-workers?" asked Tabby.

"I mostly leave them alone," said Jon. "Aside from you. And Mel. I don't really talk to many of them. I mean, it's not that I don't want to—"

"Everyone is fucking, all the time," said Tabby, and this time Jon choked on his water, putting his hand over his mouth so he didn't do a spit take all over her. She laughed again, loudly, her laughter echoing through the mostly empty cafeteria.

He swallowed what water he could, and grabbed his napkin, wiping his hands and face.

"It's like the Olympic Village in here, Jon," said Tabby. "I swear, half my lab is screwing the other half. The world is ending, we're all in here together, most of the people here are single and stressed out. It makes sense, but I don't know how you haven't seen it."

"I guess I haven't really been paying attention," said Jon. "I'm generally not a very social person."

"But if you're worried about impropriety, I think us going on a date is okay."

Jon's heart jumped again. *Date, there it is.*

He smiled then. "Then I'd love to."

"Does tonight work?" asked Tabby.

So Jon stood in front of her door. He held a tupperware container full of brownies. She hadn't told him to bring anything, but he thought it only made sense. Tommy hadn't asked where he was going, so he hadn't brought it up. They hadn't talked much, but their uneasy, unspoken truce had held, and Jon didn't want to mess with what was working.

Tabby answered before Jon could knock again. She wore

a teal dress, that clung to her curves. He'd only seen her in lab coats and business casual. She looked stunning. She had cat eye eyeshadow on, and a dark lipstick, and he couldn't talk, his voice lost somewhere between his brain and his throat.

"I'll assume you're stunned by my beauty," she said. "What did you bring?"

"B—brownies," he said.

"Silence and chocolate, the two things I love most in a man," she said, feigning a femme fatale tone. She stared at him. "Come inside, Jon."

"I feel underdressed," he said. He had worn dress slacks and a button-down shirt, but now felt like he belonged in an office park.

"You're fine," she said. "I just wanted to get dressed up. Every day in this place feels the same. It's nice to change it up a little."

Jon walked inside, following her in. He tried not to stare at her, but he mostly failed.

"It smells great," he said. "What did you make?"

"Garlic chicken and noodles," said Tabby. "It's my mom's old recipe. Really simple, but it's one of my favorites."

"That sounds great," said Jon.

"I hope you brought your appetite," said Tabby.

Jon's stomach growled, as if on cue, and he glanced around Tabby's home. It looked very different and extremely similar to his place, both at the same time. The layout was completely different, probably catered to the needs of a single person. There was no television in the big living space, though.

"No TV?" asked Jon.

"I asked not to have one," said Tabby. "I don't really watch much. Don't worry, there's four other screens in the house. I can use one of them if I really need to watch an old movie."

"I was just curious," said Jon. "Your place is different than mine."

"Well, you have your son," said Tabby. "No dependents means less space."

"I still like it," said Jon. "But I think Shaw engineered these spaces to be likable."

"Whatever. He just copied Star Trek," said Tabby. "You ready to eat? Food's not getting warmer."

"Yeah, I'm starving," he said.

"I don't have a dining room table," she said. "But I do have this lovely bar top, with some stools."

"Good enough for me," said Jon. "I have wined and dined with kings and queens and I've slept in alleys and ate pork and beans."

Tabby laughed. "Did you come up with that?"

"No, that's a quote from the late, great Dusty Rhodes," said Jon. "The pro wrestler."

"Ah," said Tabby. "I'm not familiar."

"I watched it with my dad," said Jon. Tabby put a plate down in front of him, a roasted chicken breast coated with a garlic sauce, with a side salad and some glistening linguine. It steamed.

"Is wine okay?" she asked. "I asked for a red and they sent up this cab."

"Fine with me," said Jon.

"I know it doesn't pair but I don't like white," she said, pouring them each a glass. She set down their glasses. She sat down across from him, with a similar plate of food.

"Well, don't stand on ceremony," she said.

"You don't want to toast?" asked Jon.

She rolled her eyes. "Fiiine," she said. She raised her glass. He raised his.

"What should we toast to?" he asked.

"Oh lord," she said. "To finding happiness at the end of the world."

Jon clinked her glass and then took a swallow of the wine. He wasn't an expert, but it tasted great. He grabbed his fork and ate, blowing away steam before each bite. The garlic sauce was creamy and hearty and he couldn't believe how good it tasted.

"This is incredible," said Jon.

"You're just saying that," said Tabby.

"No, this is great," said Jon. "Give your mom kudos, when you can."

"That would be tricky," said Tabby. "She passed about ten years ago."

"Oh, I forgot—"

"It's okay, Jon," she said. "But thank you."

"I don't think the world is ending, though," said Jon. "So the toast might be slightly dishonest."

"I don't know where you were before you came down here, but it sure seemed like it where I was," said Tabby. "People were fighting in the street over toilet paper."

"That doesn't mean the end of the world," said Jon. "Isn't that why we're down here in the first place? To save everything?"

"That is why we're here," said Tabby. "But even with everything down here, I'm still not sure we can reverse the entire course of human history."

"We've progressed," said Jon.

"Yeah, until the point where we can end the world on a whim," said Tabby.

"You have to have hope."

"Is that what being a parent does to you?"

"I mean, yeah, kinda," he said. "I want Tommy to have a place to grow up in. I don't want him living in Mad Max. And therefore, I have to hope that it will get better. That Shaw and everyone down here will fix things. Or at least get us on the road to fixing things, even if it takes a long time. You alright? Being pessimistic isn't like you."

Tabby nodded. "I don't like being cynical, but it's hard. I think being down here is wearing on me."

"I haven't been sleeping much," he said.

"Me neither," said Tabby. "I'm still not used to the bed."

"I'm sure they'd give you a new one if you asked," said Jon.

"The bed itself is fine," said Tabby. "It's just the environment. It's not normal, no matter how much Shaw tries to make it feel comfortable."

"Hopefully we won't be down here forever."

"I hope not," said Tabby. "I need the sun again. Vitamin D lights aren't the same thing."

"How's your work coming?" asked Jon.

"It's fine," said Tabby. "I think we're on the edge of a breakthrough, but I've felt like that before and nothing ever came. But we're close to something, even if it's failure and starting over. You?"

Jon shook his head. "Nothing. Failure after failure."

"Sorry," said Tabby.

"It's okay," said Jon. "It's just frustrating. There was always the thought in my head, that if I had more resources, more money, more lab space, an assistant, et cera, that I would get the answers. But now I have that stuff, and still nothing."

"Your work isn't easy," said Tabby. "I can't imagine all the variables."

"The supercomputers that Shaw has eliminates a lot of them, but we still can't crack it. There's something we're missing. The magic bullet is there somewhere."

"Not sure if that's the best analogy."

"It'll have to do."

"I don't think I've ever asked you," said Tabby. "Why limb regeneration?"

"Oh," said Jon. He took a breath.

"You don't have to tell me," said Tabby.

"No," said Jon, waving her off. "It's fine. I did it because of Tommy. I—he—we were in an accident. A car accident. He lost his legs, when he was little."

"Oh, I'm so sorry," said Tabby.

"It's alright," said Jon. "I don't talk about it a lot. I was still trying to figure out what I would do, and then it happened, and I pivoted toward that. It gave me purpose. It gave me drive. Too much, probably."

"How does he feel about being down here?" asked Tabby.

"Oh, he hates it," said Jon. "He wants to be up top, with his mom. But she wanted him down here."

"Did you invite her?" asked Tabby, after a pause.

"I did," said Jon. "We're just friends now. No going back. But she's a nurse, and she'd go insane down here, not being able to help, knowing that people needed it. So she said no."

"Must be hard on Tommy," said Tabby.

"It is," said Jon. "I've never been great with him. Even

before the accident. But I just want him to be safe."

"Well, nowhere safer than down here," said Tabby. "You must have been hungry."

Jon's plate was empty.

"It was just that good," said Jon. He felt his face flush as he finished the wine.

"You want more?" asked Tabby.

"Which?"

"Either," said Tabby.

"I'll have another glass of wine," said Jon.

Tabby downed the rest of her glass and poured them both another, dropping their dishes in the sink.

She raised her glass this time, and Jon met it. "To a better world," she said.

"Hear hear," he said. A pleasant buzz filled him. The wine had started its work on him.

"Sorry for being a downer," said Tabby.

"It's okay," said Jon. "It ebbs and flows. We'll make it through this. We have to."

Tabby moved around the bar top and sat next to him, her legs pressed up against his. He felt her warmth through the fabric of the pants. Her touch felt nice.

She smiled. "I'm glad you're here. It's been nice getting to know you."

"If I'm honest, you're usually the highlight of my day," he said.

"Really?" she asked.

"Yeah," he said. "The time with you is solace from the lab—"

Tabby kissed him then, putting her drink down, her lips softly pressed again his. He kissed her back, their tongues softly touching.

"Sorry," she said, breaking away.

"You don't have to apologize for that," he said.

She kissed him again, and this time he was prepared. They both stood, and she pressed herself against him, and he felt her warmth again, feel her body. His hands went to her hips, holding tight to her, afraid to let go.

She started pulling him to her bedroom.

"Are you sure?" he asked, breathless.

"The world is ending, Jon," she said, with a sly smile. "I don't feel like waiting any longer."

She kissed him again, and pulled him to her bed, and he didn't resist. Her touch was a welcome respite.

9

"How many moments in our lives are you going to miss?"

Jon stared at Maya. It was late, later than usual. He had been at the lab for eighteen hours, had gotten there before dawn, and had left after midnight. He would crawl into bed and do the same tomorrow. It had been his routine for months now. His body would occasionally give up and he'd crash for a day, sleeping for sixteen hours straight, but there were no days off. Every day was important if he was going to get the grant, because without the grant he'd be out of a job.

"I told Tommy that we'd do something this weekend," said Jon, trying to keep his voice down. "He said that'd be fine."

"He's nine years old, Jon, and he desperately wants your approval, so of course he said it'd be fine. But you didn't see him today. All his friends, all giving him presents, and not one of them could break him out of his funk. He was a hound dog all day because you weren't there. One day, one day out of hundreds, and you couldn't be there."

Jon tried to speak, but instead of saying something hurtful, he shook his head and turned around. He turned back.

"I'm doing this all for him," said Jon.

"Are you?" asked Maya. Jon remembered the look in her eyes at this moment. It would be there, every time he didn't want to remember what had happened to his marriage, how the woman he loved had finally had enough, when he tried to sleep in a bed alone every night for months, but he couldn't fall asleep because all he saw was that expression in her eyes. A look of disbelief, of exhaustion, of betrayal. It was his wife's resolve finally breaking.

"Yes, of course I am," said Jon.

"No, you're not," she said. "Tommy is fine. He's happy. He's a smart kid, with a lot of friends. His life is fine. You're doing it for *you*."

"I'm working myself to the bone, Maya," he said, his voice was louder now, and soon, soon Tommy would come into the room, and ask what was wrong, and the argument would end without resolution, but the cracks had formed, and no matter what they did, they couldn't be patched after that.

"For what?" asked Maya. "For what? For Tommy? Because he just wants to spend time with his dad. He doesn't want new legs. He just wants to see you. If you need to help him, stop this. Slow down. Forgive yourself!"

He gritted his teeth, feeling himself on the verge of tears, his face hot. He wanted to scream and yell, but then

Tommy came in, just like Jon remembered, but he wasn't in his wheelchair, he was walking.

What? That's impossible.

Tommy stood in the shadow of the doorway, obscured by darkness, but there was no wheelchair there.

"What's wrong?" he asked, and he stepped into the dim light of the bedroom, and oh god, something was wrong.

He stood on inhuman legs, distended bone and muscle, bloated, twitching, bleeding from their inhumanity. They weren't meant to be, they couldn't work, muscles didn't work like that, but they did here, and Tommy walked in on them, somehow.

"I'm wrong, daddy," said Tommy, his voice no longer his, his voice mutating, just like the rest of him, his whole body contorting, growing, distending, muscles bursting through the skin, growing, growing, growing

Oh god, let me out, let me out, LET ME OUT

Jon woke to the sound of an alarm, blaring. A recorded female voice filled the room.

EMERGENCY LOCKDOWN IN EFFECT

EMERGENCY LOCKDOWN IN EFFECT

STAY CALM

STAY CALM

EMERGENCY LOCKDOWN IN EFFECT

Jon blinked, sitting up, trying to wake himself up, struggling to shake off the nightmare, although he seemed to have woken to a new one. The lights were on, LEDs that lined every room, a dim red hue added to them he hadn't seen before.

Tommy.

Jon jumped out of bed and ran to Tommy's room. Tommy sat up in his bed, about to push himself into his wheel-chair.

"What's going on, Dad?" he asked, transitioning with practiced ease.

"I don't know," said Jon. Tommy was safe, and their home seemed normal, aside from the red lights. He went to the front door to poke his head out and see if anyone knew anything. But the door was locked, and no matter how hard he tried to open it, it wouldn't budge.

Emergency lockdown. *I guess that means we can't go anywhere.*

"We can check the raw camera feeds," said Tommy, wheeling himself out of his room.

"Right," said Jon. He forgot about them, the cameras everywhere, but they were accessible on the Shawnet. They were mostly extremely boring, with people standing around, or sitting on computers. But maybe somewhere they could see the source of all the trouble.

Jon grabbed a tablet and turned it on, flicking through the screens until he got into the Shawnet, into the camera feeds. There were thousands of cameras.

"Pull up the multi-feed," said Tommy.

"I haven't—"

"Let me do it," said Tommy, grabbing the tablet, and swiping through menu after menu until tiny squares covered the screen, each a different camera. Most of them were empty labs, or hallways, devoid of people or movement. Tommy scrolled down through the feeds, looking for any sign of deviation.

"There!" said Jon, pointing at a sudden movement in one feed.

"Problem Solving," said Tommy, and touched the feed with his finger. The feed blew up, filling the screen of the tablet.

Flames licked at the corners of the screen. There was a fire in Problem Solving. People were running in, and carrying out bodies, wielding fire extinguishers, spraying the flames. Tommy cycled between different cameras, all showing various levels of destruction in Problem Solving.

"What happened?" asked Tommy.

"I don't know," said Jon. "An accident, I guess."

They watched the camera feeds for a few minutes longer, but nothing more was revealed. The lockdown was lifted an hour later, but the adrenaline had worn off, and they both went back to sleep. The emergency had taken Jon's mind off his nightmare and sleep came easily.

An email awaited Jon in the morning, for an all hands meeting at the cafeteria at noon, sent by Sabrina.

Jon got there early, and sat next to Tabby, who had saved him a seat.

"Have you heard what's up?" asked Jon. People filtered in as they talked. Jon had never seen this many in the lunchroom. A buzz filled the air.

"Only rumors," said Tabby. "Shaw is coming up to talk to us."

"Something must have happened," said Jon. "I saw a fire on the video feed."

"It was more than a fire," said Tabby. "It had to have been, for the man himself to talk to us. For all of us to be here."

Shaw walked in at exactly noon, trailed by Sabrina. He stood in front of the assembled scientists, sitting throughout the cafeteria, and more standing behind them. The group hushed.

"Hello," he said. "I wanted us all to gather so that I could speak to the emergency lockdown last night. I don't like taking you away from your work, or leaving my own, but this is a necessary step."

"Last night, the FUTURE lab was a victim of sabotage. Dr. Armitage in Problem Solving planted a small firebomb in the lab, near a supply of flammable materials. As far as we can tell, he had hoped to set off an inferno, destroying the work of the Problem Solving lab. He failed."

Silence hung in the air. Everyone's eyes looked at Shaw.

"The fire was contained, with only slight injuries for a few people working late. Smoke inhalation and minor burns. They will recover. Some are already back at work. I would expect nothing less from the group of determined and talented people we have here."

"Dr. Armitage wouldn't speak to his allegiances, but we suspect he was sent down here as part of an anarcho-terrorist group that has been attacking my holdings on the surface. I don't know how long Armitage has been a member of them, or when he switched sides, but he certainly meant to harm us, and ruin our work down here. It was a despicable deed, not only for seeking to hurt some of our team, but for attempting to sabotage our work, transformative discoveries that could save the world. They would destroy them."

Shaw swept his vision across the assembled scientists.

"Armitage was a saboteur, and should have never have been invited down here. That mistake was mine, and I want to apologize publicly to all of you for allowing it to happen. I would say that it won't happen again—"

Shaw stopped again, his face sterner now, looking over

them, his eyes hard.

"But I don't know that," said Shaw. "Last night revealed that our vetting measures weren't as air tight as I thought they were. I had hoped that everyone here could be trusted. But that is obviously not the case. There could be more, situated among us. People who have hidden like snakes in the grass, waiting for their moment to strike, to hurt or kill, to destroy and demolish. Keep your eyes open. Watch for deception. Report any suspicious behavior to your pillar lead."

Shaw paused. "Any questions, before we end the meeting?"

Silence hung again. Jon had a lot of questions, but he didn't know if now was the best time to ask them. One question was at the forefront of his mind, and he almost asked, but luckily someone else spoke up, a doctor he didn't recognize.

"Where is Dr. Armitage now?" he asked.

Shaw turned to him. "You worked with him, didn't you, Alan?"

"Yes," said the man.

"I'm sorry for that," said Shaw. "But you're capable. We still have all of his research. But Armitage himself has been cast out. Along with his wife and two children. They have been exiled from the FUTURE lab, thrown back to the wolves. He deserved worse, and I considered it, but in the end, it's adequate punishment. To be cast out from paradise. Any other questions?"

There were none then, or at least no one who wanted to ask them.

"Then we will end with that," said Shaw. "Let's get back to work, and put this unfortunate incident behind us. Stay vigilant." And Shaw was gone, back out the door, with Sabrina right behind him.

The group dispersed, returning to the elevators to get back to work. Others went to grab lunch. Jon sat with Tabby, waiting for others to leave.

"What do you make of that?" asked Jon.

"I don't know," said Tabby. "I met Armitage once, when he came to Energy for some help with his project. Seemed like a nice guy. Seemed earnest."

"That's what everyone says about someone, after they find out they're a bad guy," said Jon.

"Yeah, I guess," said Tabby. "What did Shaw mean when he said he cast him out? Did he send him home? Or does that literally mean kick him out the door and abandon him and his family up top, wherever we are?"

"Canada," said Jon. "Tommy guessed somewhere in Northern Canada."

"Not a bad one," said Tabby. "But I doubt it's somewhere hospitable."

"I don't know," said Jon. "He tried to destroy the place. People could have been hurt."

"Yeah," said Tabby. "That's true. I still feel bad for him, regardless of what he did."

"At least everyone's okay," said Jon. "And none of the work got damaged."

"True," said Tabby. He could see she still had other thoughts, something she wasn't sharing, but he didn't push. If she wanted to tell him, she would, without prodding.

"Will I see you tonight?" asked Jon.

Tabby sighed. "No," she said. "We're really close to re-sults, so we're trying to push to get it done tonight. Or at least see if we failed tonight. Sorry."

"It's okay," said Jon. "I understand. I'd be doing the same."

"You'll get there," said Tabby. "I need to go." She kissed him, and then she was gone.

Jon returned to work and tried to focus as they repeated their experiments. They waited to see if this time, the rats would regrow their limbs, without mutation, without the horror.

But his thoughts returned to Dr. Armitage. Of his family being abandoned on the surface. And of Shaw's worse punishment.

10

Jon felt the tension in his chest. The heat sunk down from his face into his heart. The rage simmered there, and he put down the scalpel, grabbing a clipboard with a clutched hand. He squeezed it with all his might, but the metal didn't bend or break, and so he threw it. The clipboard smashed against the far wall with a CLUNG, and then smacked to the ground. Neither were damaged.

Mel winced, squeezing herself together, waiting to see if Jon would throw anything else. Jon didn't, only sitting down on a small lab stool, his head in his hands.

"Are you okay?" she asked, finally.

"I'm sorry," said Jon. "I shouldn't have done that. I'm just so frustrated."

It had been weeks since the meeting, weeks full of testing more and more serums, with more and more rats, all of them failures. All he saw behind his eyelids were mutated limbs and sedated animals, dissected to reveal nothing of value. Over and over again.

"I am too," said Mel.

"I don't know what to do," said Jon.

"We can try changing the delivery system again," said Mel. "Maybe if we switch back to the virus—"

"I really don't think it's that," said Jon. "We've tried switching so many variables, and nothing is changing, not drastically. I think it's a more foundational problem."

"Meaning?" asked Mel.

"I don't know," said Jon. "I've been trying to figure it out, but there is just no consistency. It's maddening."

Jon sighed. He thought back to Shaw's words, of wanting results within a year's time, and Jon would be lucky if he had gotten anything positive within that time span. It had been almost two months, and there was zero progress. He felt the pressure building up behind him. He hadn't seen Tabby in weeks, aside from a quick lunch together here and there. He hadn't heard from Maya either. He had continued to send her letters, and he hoped she was getting them. Tommy had settled into a routine and luckily had made a friend to play games with. It was the only silver lining.

"I'm going to get some water," said Jon. He grabbed his bottle, to refill at the cooler, and headed toward it, out through his lab doors. The glass defrosted, and he walked. He turned the corner and saw the cooler.

Fuck.

Stone stood next to it, refilling his bottle as well, drinking from it before putting it back under the spigot. Jon thought to back off, to retreat, and wait for Stone to go back to his lab, but then he dismissed the notion. He wouldn't run away. He wasn't a child. He would get his water, and he would return to work.

Jon attempted a smile as Stone looked at him approaching, before putting his bottle under the other spigot, filling it. Stone towered over him.

"What was that noise I heard coming from your lab?" asked Stone, his deep voice humming. "I hope everything's okay."

"Everything is fine," said Jon. "Just dropped something, and it knocked some stuff over."

"That's not what I've heard, though," said Stone. "That everything is fine. I've heard you've gotten absolutely zero results in what, almost two months?"

Jon said nothing, only stared at the water level of his bottle.

Fill, goddamnit, fill.

"The Chosen One isn't getting it done," said Stone. "It really is a pity. Thought for sure you'd be in the special project lab by now. Shaw would have made sure of it, right? You are his pet, after all."

That same heat returned in Jon's chest. He squeezed his metal water bottle. He tried to breathe, to take control of his breath and his temper, but it resisted.

"But I guess he can't do that unless you give him *something*, right? He can't play favorites if you're obviously incompetent," said Stone.

Jon gritted his teeth, his bottle almost full. "I notice that you're still in this lab as well," said Jon. "I don't really know how your research is doing, though. I don't spend my time watching other people's work. I mostly focus on my own." Jon stood up, staring Stone in the eyes. Stone stared back.

"Some of us have to earn our way," said Stone. "It takes more time. It's harder. You wouldn't know about that, being the pet and all. I mean, if I had gotten nothing in two months, I'd probably be out of here altogether. But here you are. Still chasing your pipe dreams."

Jon fumed, but said nothing. He forced himself to turn around and return to his lab. He was giving Stone exactly what he wanted. The only thing that would shut him up would be results. He felt Stone's eyes on him from behind, but he didn't give him the satisfaction of looking back, closing the doors behind him, the glass frosting.

"That son of a bitch," said Jon, under his breath.

"That damn water cooler," said Mel, sitting at her workstation. "That bastard."

Jon sighed and finally cracked a slight smile. "It's Stone. He was waiting there, like a bird of prey, ready to swoop down and pepper me with insults."

"Yes," said Mel. "All those hawks and falcons. They sure are cutting with their words."

"Okay, well maybe my metaphor wasn't perfect," said Jon. "But he's so infuriating. I want to hit him."

"I wouldn't do that," said Mel. "Unless you have some secret fighting skill that I'm not aware of."

"No," said Jon. "I've never been in a fight."

"I don't believe it," said Mel, dryly.

"Very funny," said Jon. "What were we doing?"

"I think we were crying into our hands, lamenting our existence," said Mel.

"No—" but then Jon's phone buzzed in his pocket. He

pulled it out to see Sabrina's name on the screen. He answered.

"Hello, Jon Matthews," he said.

"Hello, Doctor," said Sabrina, her voice clear. "Mr. Shaw requests your presence."

"When?" asked Jon.

"As soon as possible," said Sabrina.

"I'll be right there," said Jon, and the call ended.

"Who was that?" asked Mel.

"Shaw wants to see me," said Jon. Jon's mind went to Dr. Armitage, exiled on the surface. Of Stone's recent words. But more than that, his thoughts went to the failures of his research in the lab.

Mel tried to force a smile, but largely failed. "Good luck."

Shaw stood as Jon entered, extending his metallic hand, just like the first time. Jon shook it, shockingly cold to the touch.

"Thanks for coming on such short notice, Jon," said Shaw. He smiled and sat back down behind his desk. He gestured to a chair in front of it, and Jon sat.

"No problem," said Jon. "It is your show." Jon sat there, trying to dispel the well of anxiety that had opened in his stomach.

"I hear you've been having some trouble," said Shaw.

"Yes," said Jon. "You could say that."

"Tell me about it," said Shaw. "What's the problem?"

"I don't really know," said Jon. "The problem is I can't identify the problem. We have the computer modeling thousands of different serums, and we experiment with the ones with the highest probability of success. We dissect our failures, use it to change the models, and move on. And that should, given enough time, gear the models toward progress. Or at least some measure of it. It should get us closer to success, at least. But nothing. We've only had failure. The rats haven't gotten any closer to regeneration. They've regrown the limb, certainly, but nothing approximating the original limb, and it takes hours."

"So they are regenerating?" asked Shaw.

"Of a sort," said Jon. "They're regrowing tissue, but it's nothing like their original limbs. It's muscle and bone with no rhyme or reason. The rats would be crippled for life. Worse than with no limb at all. It doesn't make sense. The rat's DNA is programmed with the original schematic for its arm. It's how it was formed in the womb in the first place. I've tried tinkering with CRISPR, but I honestly don't think it's that at all. The science is sound."

"Then where does the problem lie?" asked Shaw.

"I—I don't know," said Jon.

Shaw waved him off. "Don't give me that," said Shaw. "You suspect something, I know you do. You're a smart man, Jon. Your results are all inconclusive, so ignore them. What does your gut say is the problem?"

Jon looked at Shaw.

"My gut says we're overloading the body of the rat," said Jon. "Because it can't heal at the rate we are telling it to. That no matter how many calories we pump into it, it simply can't absorb them as fast as we need, and can't deliver them to the wound site as quickly as we need. The wound is healing yes, but because it's healing too slowly, the regenerated limb is abnormal and deformed. I should probably slow it down. Go back and start—"

"No," said Shaw. "Slowing down is the opposite of what

we want. Is there any way you can speed up the metabolism of the animal? So that it can absorb the nutrients faster?"

"Once you fiddle with the metabolic systems, you are creating new problems, ones you don't want to have to solve, things worse than losing a limb. Because you're going back, and re-writing genetic code after you've done your initial work, and god knows what will be un-done successfully."

"So, you need the rat to absorb nutrients faster, to facilitate the regeneration process? Do you think that if you could deliver those extra nutrients to the wound site, the reconstruction process would work?"

"Yes," said Jon. "That's what my gut says."

"Hmm," said Shaw. "Give me a moment." Shaw hit a control and a thin screen slid up from somewhere in his desk. He slid his hands across it a few times, studying something.

"Have you considered asking some of your colleagues for help?"

"No," said Jon. "I've thought about it, but I've never been good at asking for assistance. And we're all so busy. I don't want to take someone's time away from their own research."

"Well, then I insist," said Shaw. "I think that in this case, it will be beneficial, to both of you. You know how much I want your research to bear fruit, Jon, and you need to take that next step before I can push you up into the special projects lab. But with help, I think you can get there, and move your experiments to the next level."

"If you think it's best," said Jon. "Who do you suggest I work with?"

"Dr. Stone," said Shaw. "His research seems catered to work with yours. I see you as two puzzle pieces, that when locked together, will create a larger picture."

"Dr. Stone?" asked Jon. Jon remembered Stone's dead stare at him earlier. The insults. "I—"

"Is there a problem, Jon?" asked Shaw, his eyes fixed on Jon's. The jovial and conversational tone that Shaw had until this moment seemed to die on the vine, the room suddenly feeling cold and alien. Jon thought to his failures.

"No, of course not," said Jon. "I'll speak to Dr. Stone about his work, and see how he can help me."

"It's a two-way street," said Shaw. "I think you can help him as well. You'll make an impressive pair. The two of you together will be dynamite."

11

Shaw was right about Stone. Jon hadn't looked at his research, had avoided it altogether, because he didn't want to
be like Stone. He preferred not to obsess over someone else's
results, good or bad. He didn't want to be that person.

But if he had looked at Stone's research earlier, he might
have swallowed his pride and asked for his help before Shaw
intervened, because Shaw was right. They were like puzzle
pieces.

Stone was researching advanced healing processes as
well, which made sense. They were both in the Medical pillar and accelerated healing was a utilitarian approach that
would help people. Maybe that was why Stone disliked him
so much. Because he thought Jon was trying to steal his
thunder.

Stone's research, at a glance, was seeking to utilize the hagfish's ability to absorb nutrients through its skin. He would find out what made it tick, how it made that ability work, and then port it over to humans, so they could absorb nutrients faster, by being put in a nutrient bath or something similar. But it also didn't broach how to speed up the healing like Jon had tackled. And it was on a smaller scale, only attempting to heal normal wounds quickly. It made sense for them to combine their effort.

That fact didn't make Jon feel any better. He went back to the lab after talking to Shaw with anxiety in his gut. He had never enjoyed the social aspects of his work, like applying for grants and social networking, necessary things for any occupation, but nothing he liked. And it had cost him, frankly. No matter how hard he tried, his heart wasn't in it, and people could tell. They wanted a smiling face to give their money to, not some awkward conversation about amputated limbs.

Still, Jon thought to Shaw's eyes when Jon showed reticence, and they reminded him of the same look he had when he announced Armitage had been exiled. Stone had been exaggerating when he spoke of being thrown out for not getting results, but the idea still worried Jon.

And so he went to Stone's lab, taking deep breaths as he approached, keeping himself calm, preparing himself to ask Stone for help. The doors were closed. Jon pushed the doorbell, so to speak, waiting for a response.

Stone's assistant answered the door.

"Hi, how can I help you?" he asked, smiling.

"I'd like to talk to Dr. Stone," said Jon. He glanced over the assistant's shoulder, and saw Stone at his workstation.

Stone looked over his own shoulder and glanced at Jon before looking back at his work.

"Ah, Dr. Stone is in the middle of something right now, so if you could come back—"

"Let him in, Andrew," said Stone. "I'm curious why the Chosen One would appear at my doorstep."

Andrew stepped aside and let Jon through. Jon walked in, Stone's lab noticeably smaller than his, although set up similarly. Stone continued to look at his work on his screen even as Jon approached him, standing next to him as Stone sat.

"Pull up a chair, Jon," said Stone, still not looking at him. Jon looked around and grabbed one, pulling it near Stone. Stone let him sit there for a solid thirty seconds before he finally looked away from the monitor, his same cold eyes analyzing Jon now.

"Why are you here?" asked Stone.

Jon took a deep breath. He had a strategy, and he would stick to it, no matter how much it irked him. "I need your help."

Stone smiled, a genuine smile, a shark's smile, revealing all his white teeth. "You need *my* help? Really?"

"Yes," said Jon. "I think your research is the key to unlocking results from mine. If we combine—"

"Why on Earth would I help you cannibalize my work?" asked Stone, cutting him off.

"It wouldn't be cannibalizing your work," said Jon. "We would combine our research, so both of us could reach our goals. Together. Shaw—"

"Less than a minute in and you're already throwing his name around," said Stone. "I thought it would take longer, but you're already proving my point. I'm not trying to chase vanity projects, I'm looking for—"

"Would you let me finish?" asked Jon. "I'm trying to help—"

"I don't need your help," said Stone, raising his voice, his deep bellow filling the room.

"You don't?" asked Jon. "Are you sure? You went on and on about how I haven't gotten any results, but I know you've noticed, just like I've noticed, that there are more and more empty labs around here. More and more of our colleagues are being called up to the big leagues while both of us are still putzing around in the minors. I know you want to be down there, just like I do. Because as much as Shaw doesn't say, the threat of getting kicked out of here is real, even for me."

Stone looked at him, and Jon saw that he actually was considering him now. "Go on."

"Shaw told me to approach you, to ask you to partner with me, and I don't think he did it for no reason at all. Shaw does everything for a reason, and you and I both know that he's personally invested in my success. He desperately wants me to succeed, and you're a card he hasn't played yet to ensure it. And I realize you don't like me, but I don't care. I want my research to work, and I want to be in the special projects lab, because I want to stay down here where it's safe, and I want my son down here where it's safe. And you do, too. And I think you can help me, and I think I can help you. I'll acknowledge that Shaw wants me here for no damn good reason except he wants his arm back, but that's the very reason you should be my partner. Because if you do, and we succeed, you and your research comes to the special projects lab with me. You become a Chosen One as well."

Stone looked at him a moment longer. "Two conditions. First, I get equal credit, for whatever we do. Two, you ensure I get into the dark lab, no matter what Shaw says. You make sure I get in. You do that, I'm game."

"Done," said Jon, meeting Stone's eyes.

"Okay," said Stone, nodding. "Let's get to work."

*

"And it was like a switch flipped in him or something," said Jon. He laid next to Tabby in her bedroom. "Openly antagonistic toward me, and then, as soon as he agrees to help, he's Mr. Helpful. Sure, still a little curt, but like a totally different guy."

"He sees you as an asset now," said Tabby. "I've known plenty of people like that. As soon as they either see you as someone they can use, or something that benefits them, they turn, really quick. He's hitching his wagon to you. He knows that insulting you now won't get him anywhere. He probably still doesn't like you, if that makes you feel any better."

"It doesn't, really, but thanks anyway," said Jon.

He hadn't seen her alone in weeks, but she had invited him over tonight, and he had leapt at the chance. Spending time with her now, he realized how much he had missed her. They had barely finished dinner before they had moved into the bedroom.

"Make any progress with him today?" she asked.

"No, nothing yet," said Jon. "But we spent most of the time organizing our data. Mel took charge on it. We're moving to a shared lab space tomorrow. I'm hoping we'll start seeing results soon. I'm worried if we don't."

"You'll get results. You both are very smart. You'll crack it, especially with Stone's help."

"I don't want Tommy to be left out in the cold," said Jon.

"I don't think Shaw would kick you out, regardless," said Tabby.

"I'm not sure," said Jon. "I still think about what you said about Armitage."

"Armitage is the exception," said Tabby. "Nothing else has happened since, and I think Shaw has settled down. The attack really flustered him."

"We need results soon if we want to get into the special projects lab," said Jon. Tabby said nothing, her eyes suddenly looking everywhere but him.

"What's wrong?" asked Jon. He'd seen her enough to know when something was up.

Tabby looked at him, meeting his eyes. "Well, part of the reason I invited you over is because I finally broke through on my research. We got a working prototype of the battery pack."

"That's great!" said Jon. "Congratulations!"

"Thanks," said Tabby. "But I talked to Shaw, one-on-one. I see what you mean, about him, now. He invited me to the special projects lab. I wanted to tell you."

"Well, that's fantastic," said Jon. "I'm proud of you."

"I just—I just don't know how much I'll see of you," said Tabby. "I've—I've really enjoyed getting to know you, being with you. Whatever we are—I like it a lot. But—but I don't know—"

"Hey," he said, softly caressing her face. "It's okay. I understand."

"I don't want to break up with you—I mean, I'm not

even your girlfriend, technically, but you know—I'm just worried—"

"We don't have to label this," said Jon. "But if it's what you want, I'd like to still see you, when we can wrangle it, while we're down here. And if we can manage it, when we're back up top. How does that sound?"

"That sounds reasonable," said Tabby. "Christ, I don't usually get butterflies in my stomach, but Jesus, trying to tell you—"

Jon laughed. "Are you excited to move to the other lab?"

"Sort of," she said. "I've heard rumors about it. I'm sure you have too. About how projects escalate when they get there."

"What do you mean?" asked Jon.

"I know someone in Systems who went down there," said Tabby. "I've only talked to him one time since he transferred, and he said it's way less about proof of concept anymore. It's not proving a hypothesis. It's about real world applications. It gets way more serious. It's prepping the tech for people to use."

"Well, I assumed that would happen at some point along the line," said Jon.

"Yeah, I guess that's true," said Tabby. "But the speed. It's happening so fast."

"Shaw wants to use this stuff while he still can," said Jon. "I don't blame him, I guess. Get it out there while there's still people to save. Did you hear anything else?"

"Not really," said Tabby. "He was kind of tight-lipped about it. There was one thing that stood out, though."

"What was it?"

"He said security is way more strict," she said. "There's

actually guards down there, not just cameras."

"Guarding against who?" asked Jon.

"I don't know," said Tabby. "I'm guessing people like Dr. Armitage. The projects are further along down there, so it would be easier to steal and implement, if they got out with it. And sabotage would be that much disastrous."

"Then they're defending against that," said Jon.

"I'm just nervous," said Tabby. "I feel like it's the night before the first day of school, and I don't know anyone, or any of the teachers, but this time, I've got to do a report with my whole life on the line."

"I don't think your life is on the line," said Jon. "And you're smarter than anyone else here. You'll do great."

"I'm glad someone thinks so," said Tabby. "I'll try and carve out time for us."

"So will I," said Jon. "Tommy hasn't said anything about me spending time here, and I hope his silence is consent. Not that I need it—"

"But you'd like it," said Tabby. "I get it. You could just ask him."

"I know," said Jon. "But he finally seems like he's comfortable down here. I don't want to poke the bear."

"Fair enough," said Tabby.

"God, I'm tired," he said. "Sleep has been hard to come by."

"Why?"

"I keep having nightmares," said Jon. "Makes it hard to get back to sleep."

"Don't worry," she said. "I'll keep them away." And then she pressed against him, and she kissed him, and the rest of the world melted away.

12

"We can't do that. We can't just push it harder," said Jon. He sat across from Stone in their lab. They'd been working together for a week, and things were finally coming to a head.

"We have to, Jon," said Stone. "We're still not getting anywhere. We have to ramp up the accelerator."

Jon shook his head. "It's a rat, not a car. And even in a car, if you accelerate too fast, too hard, you'll overdrive the engine and it'll burn up. We'll burn up the damn rat before it even gets started healing. It'll die before its arm regenerates."

They hadn't run any experiments for the entire week, spending the time organizing their new lab, getting their ducks in a row, and deciding on how to simulate their models. Mel had coded it all, and they'd gotten results back, adding in Stone's research. Nothing in the models looked substantially different from Jon's original ones, and that worried him.

"What are you so worried about?" asked Stone. "It's just a damn rat. We've killed thousands of them. If one burns up, we'll alter the code and try again. We don't have the benefit of time right now. We have to move."

"Just because we have access to all the rats in the world doesn't mean we should treat them as disposable. The moment we ignore any kind of unnecessary pain—"

"They won't be in pain, they're sedated!" said Stone, standing up.

"That's not the point," said Jon. "Sit down." Stone stared at him, and then sat again.

"We want to—no, we *need* to be smart here," said Jon. "We can't just churn through rats searching heedlessly for a solution. We want to maximize every rat, every test, every moment we have. Because the clock is ticking. Okay? We will move quickly, but we will do it with purpose. What is our goal?"

Stone stared at him. "Why—"

"What is our goal?"

"Right now? For a rat to regenerate a limb successfully, quickly, and able to have full use of the limb after being brought out of sedation."

"Okay," said Jon. "That's our goal. How are we achieving it?"

"We'll accelerate the healing process at the wound site and convert dormant cells in the rat into stem cells, allowing them to be used as fuel to power the regeneration. In tandem, we will transform the rat's skin into a feeding mechanism, and then submerge it in a dense nutrient bath, giving it the additional fuel it needs to heal quickly, without deformity or mutation."

Jon smiled. "You make it so sound so easy."

"In theory, it is," said Stone. "But in practice, there's so many variables."

"Let's start out with our models, and see what happens," said Jon. "Maybe the skin absorption and nutrient bath will make the difference.

So they started, all four of them crowded around a single rat, under sedation. Jon removed its arm, and then Stone injected it with the magic formula. They watched as its genome was re-written, its skin softening, glistening. Stone slipped it into a nutrient bath, it's stump and mouth sticking out, but all other parts of it submerged in the milky white substance.

"How long will it take?" asked Mel in a hushed whisper.

"I don't know," said Jon, but Jon wouldn't be letting the rat out of his sight. He wanted to see what happened, even if it was incremental.

"My god," said Andrew, standing with them. The arm healed, the bones knitting themselves back together, muscles interlacing, and then they reached the point where the rat's internally stored fuel wasn't enough, and it processed the nutrient bath.

Jon wouldn't have believed it if he hadn't seen it, but the liquid level of the bath was visibly shrinking, the bath being absorbed through the rat's new skin. The arm continued to regenerate, bones and muscles forming, but then the absorption rate stalled, and Jon saw the arm tissue falter, and then mutate, with bulbous bone and muscle pushing out and through, the rat's arm no longer looking like it should.

"Fuck," said Stone. Soon the nutrient bath was gone, burned through, but only to grow a deformed, monstrous arm. "Ugh."

Jon yelled, but in happiness, whooping through the lab, pumping his arms.

"Why are you so happy?" asked Stone.

"Because this is progress!" said Jon. "My hunch was right. It's the absorption rate! It caps successful regeneration. All we have to do is up the absorption rate in its skin."

"So *I* was right," said Stone, arching his eyebrows. "We need to speed up the process."

"Well—yes," said Jon. "And this proves it. And it proves we're on the right path. We just need to fiddle."

So fiddle they did. Stone tried to accelerate all at once, but Jon preached patience, and the model Mel built spit out new formulas over the next few days.

They saw slow and steady progress, as the rats regenerated more and more of their limbs before lapsing into mutation. Stone got more and more frustrated. Jon only grew happier because they were close to success, each rat a substantial jump now.

Shaw had been right. Stone's help was all he needed to succeed. Stone was driven, and somewhat overbearing, but worked hard, and desperately wanted progress, just like Jon did. Jon's mind went to Tabby in the special projects lab. She messaged him, but they no longer saw each other at lunch, and he hadn't been over to her place since she'd moved up. He understood, but he missed her.

His thoughts would move to Maya as well, as he waited for results from the newest subject, of how she was doing top side. He hoped she was okay. He hoped she had gotten his letters.

"This is the day," said Jon. "I can feel it." It had been a week full of testing. It was Friday, technically, but the days blended together down here, the normal calendar only used as a common reference point.

"Oh, Mr. Optimism today," said Stone. "I adjusted the models to further accelerate the rat's absorption rate. It's over 300% over where we started."

"Isn't that too much?" asked Jon.

"Why am I here?" asked Stone. "You should trust me once in a while, Jon. I was right before we even started the new experiments, and I'm right now. This is the right number. Trust me."

"Okay," said Jon. "I'll trust you. I don't want to overwhelm the animal."

"It won't," said Stone. "But it's not like we're playing patty-cake with it. We're pushing the limits of biology."

We're playing God. Stone didn't say it, but they both thought it. But god didn't take away people's limbs, it was bombs, and bullets, and accidents, and Jon thought back to the night Tommy lost his legs, and then he pushed it away.

That won't help you now. Focus on the science.

They prepped the rat, putting it under sedation, while Stone prepared the injection, the computer mixing it to the exact specifications of their model. Jon eyed it as Stone carried it over. The rat, once injected, would absorb nutrients insanely fast. Andrew stood nearby with more of the liquid nutrient bath, ready to refill as necessary.

Stone looked to Jon and nodded. Jon removed the rat's limb, blood spurting out onto prepared gauze. Mel applied pressure to the wound as Stone injected the rat with the new serum, the right mixture, the magic formula. He handed off the syringe to Mel, and he then placed the rat in the nutrient bath. Blood continued to shoot out of the wound, mixing with the nutrient bath into the dull pink of pepto bismol, but it soon stopped, as its genes changed, as it became different. Better.

Jon watched as the blood flow slowed and then stopped, the healing beginning. The rate at which it healed was incredible, matched only by the amount at which it absorbed nutrients through its skin. The nutrient bath lowered quickly, as the rat became a conduit, its body an engine, converting the liquid into stem cells into a new arm in the span of seconds.

"Andrew," said Stone, shortly, and Andrew stepped up, slowly adding more of the milky white substance into the small tub, filling it as fast as the rat could absorb it. The arm regenerated as Jon watched, bones and muscle, and then skin forming over top. No sign of mutation or deformity.

"I don't believe it," said Stone.

"It's working," said Jon.

"No, not working," said Stone. "Worked. It's done."

The level of the bath had stalled, the rat done absorbing nutrients, its body back at equilibrium. The arm had regenerated fully, identical to the limb Jon had removed minutes ago. Jon carefully touched it, and it was solid, moving and flexing just like the one it had replaced.

"Yes," said Stone, pumping his arm now.

"Wait," said Jon. "One more test. The real test. Bring it out of sedation, Mel."

Mel removed the IV, sliding it out from the rat, and

pulled it from the nutrient bath, wiping it down with a towel and placing it on the table again.

"How long?" asked Jon.

"A couple minutes," said Mel.

They all watched, waiting for the rat to show signs of life again. Would the limb work? That was the true test. A limb that looked the same but hung lifeless was no better, and Jon's mind raced between all the problems that could still be there, of misplaced nerve endings or internal mutations that would leave the arm nonfunctional.

He held his breath, and then forced himself to inhale, forcing air in.

The rat twitched then, its ears slightly moving, and then its whiskers. Its eyes opened next. The sedative wore off, its brain coming back online. Its body moved. Its breathing becoming more regular.

"Holy shit," said Jon. The rat stood up and groomed itself. Cleaning itself with the regenerated limb. It moved fully, and the rat showed no sign of distress.

"Fucking what!" said Stone.

"We did it!" yelled Jon, extending his hand to Stone. Stone shook it. Jon hugged Mel and shook Andrew's hand. The rat continued to groom itself, even as they celebrated.

Jon carefully grabbed the rat, which didn't object to him picking it up. He felt the new limb touch him, move against him. It worked. It really worked.

"Success."

13

Shaw invited Jon and Stone to meet within the hour. Neither of them had reported anything to him. They hadn't had time. They were too busy recording all their results, and planning on follow-up experiments, to fine tune the serum.

They didn't get that far, and both were in the elevator, requesting Shaw's office, a faint drop in their stomachs as the tube dropped.

"How did he know?" asked Jon.

"You really didn't think he hasn't been keeping a close eye on you?" asked Stone. "Everything else in here is abstract. Help people. Feed them, heal them. With you, it's his *arm*."

"So he's been watching," said Jon.

"Of course he has," said Stone. "And if he hasn't, he's had

someone do it for him."

They arrived at Shaw's office, and Shaw stood up to greet them, just like he had previously, but this time he avoided a handshake and stepped in to hug them both.

"I hear congratulations are in order," he said, hugging Stone, and then hugging Jon. Jon hugged him back, trying not to feel awkward, embracing the richest man on Earth. Shaw clapped him on the back and then rubbed. Jon's memory of saying talking to Shaw felt like talking to his father returned. His father would do the same thing whenever Jon had accomplished anything.

"Please, sit," said Shaw, gesturing to the chairs. He was all smiles, as much of a smile his plastic face could manage. They sat. "Can I get you anything to drink? Champagne?"

"No, that's okay," said Jon. Stone waved him off.

"So, you found success?" asked Shaw. Jon waited for Stone to answer, but Stone said nothing. Jon realized that Stone probably hadn't even met Shaw in person before.

"Yes," said Jon. "The rat regrew its limb, and it's completely functional."

"How long did it take?" asked Shaw.

"Maybe ten minutes," said Jon. "The speed was astounding."

"Incredible," said Shaw, his eyes bouncing between the two of them. "Simply incredible. I knew you could do it. And I knew Dr. Stone was just the key to getting you over the top. You add his knowledge and research to your own, and boom, success within two weeks. Simply amazing."

"You were right, Mr. Shaw," said Jon. "And now we have our first success. We're on the right road."

"I would say so!" said Shaw, perking up even more. "The

right road. Ha. You're doing a little better than just on the right road. You've achieved complete limb regeneration in a mammal in ten minutes!"

"Well, thank you," said Jon. "I just don't want to put the cart before the horse, you know. We've still got to repeat the tests, and refine our variables, make the process more efficient. After that, we can start worrying about larger—"

Shaw waved him off. "No no no, I told you Jon, stop thinking like you're still on the surface. That is the rigors of old science, *slow* science. At that pace it will be years before we find anything substantial, before we move onto human testing. We don't have time for those obsolete standards."

"I mean, that's well and good, Mr. Shaw," said Jon. "But we still don't know if the rat's long-term health is affected. The limb could stop functioning tomorrow and we would be back where we started—"

"Tut tut," said Shaw. "There is always risk whenever you are pushing science to the limit, pressing the human body to the limit. And frankly, I think it's time to move on from rat testing, to larger animals. To get us closer to humans."

"Well, I was going to plan on either cats or dogs next, or maybe pigs if we're feeling really audacious—"

"No," said Shaw, interrupting him again. "Chimps. I want you to move onto chimps."

Jon reflexively shook his head. He felt Stone staring at him, trying to tell him to agree with his eyes, but Jon wouldn't go along with some plan he didn't believe in. "That's out of the question, Mr. Shaw. Chimps are much more complicated than rats. Their autonomous systems alone—there's no way we can just port over our same experiment and expect it to work. The manpower alone needed to program the models. Mel would have to work twelve-hour days for months."

"I know that, Jon," said Shaw. "That's why I'm moving you and your team to the special projects lab. Where you'll have more assistants. A much larger team. You and Dr. Stone will be less hands-on, and be in a more managerial role. Delegating tasks, and overseeing research, but not doing it directly. Frankly, you're too valuable to be wasting time down in the trenches. Even your assistants will be given a wider purview. It's a promotion in the truest sense of the word."

Shaw stared at him, the same smile on his face, but Jon felt the menace behind his eyes. Shaw wanted the project to move forward, and he wanted it quickly. Jon knew he should agree to it all, and worry about his ethics later, but his heart spoke before his mind could stop him.

"I don't know if I'm comfortable with that, Mr. Shaw," said Jon. "Pushing the research too hard and too far, too quickly is dangerous."

Shaw didn't change his look, but Jon felt Stone's eyes on him. "Jon, there's no moving backward here," said Shaw. "The only way forward is in the special projects lab. You realize that by now. You want to advance your research, don't you?"

And before Jon could say anything, Stone interrupted him.

"Of course, Mr. Shaw," said Stone. "I, for one, am excited to work in a new lab with even more resources. I'm sure we'll able to find more success, now that we've cracked the problem. We don't want to stagnate in the Medical pillar, do we, Jon?" Jon looked to Stone at the mention of his name, and Stone's eyes were cold and hard, and told Jon to agree at any cost, asked him if he was a complete idiot, told him of course you agree to move into the special projects lab, Eaton Shaw is not a person you say no to. Jon took a heavy breath and stowed his ethics back into his heart.

"I—of course, Mr. Shaw," said Jon. "I don't mean to sound critical. I just—I just want to make sure we succeed."

Shaw smiled again, and the menace vanished, tucked deep inside. "Of course, Jon. I understand. It's your baby. Don't worry, we will succeed. I guarantee it."

"That sounds great, Mr. Shaw," said Stone.

"You'll have a new lab space tomorrow," said Shaw. "With a tour of the lab. I suggest you talk to your assistants and then take the rest of the day off. To take a breath and re-vitalize yourself. Because tomorrow, the real work begins."

And the meeting was over, and they were in the elevator.

"What the hell was that?" asked Stone as soon as the doors closed.

"What do—"

"Shaw is offering us a spot in the special projects lab, and you throw it back in his face? Oh no, I don't want more re-sources, no, I don't want to be the golden goose—"

"He's moving us way too fast," said Jon. "It's going to cause us headaches."

"Who fucking cares?" asked Stone. "More problems than us getting thrown the fuck out of here? You do realize that Shaw has all your research, right? Mine too? It's all in his computers, and if we get tossed, along with your son, that research ain't coming with us. He'll keep it and use it any-way. So pull your head out of your ass and just do what he says. Smile and like it."

"I—"

"I know, you're an idiot," said Stone. "Believe me, I understand. I'd like a nice safe spot down here while the world is ending, so try and play nice with the billionaire."

And then the elevator stopped, back on the Medical pillar, and Stone walked out. Jon followed him. Mel was happy to be moving on, and even happier at the news she'd be getting more responsibilities. He helped her pack up the few things he wanted to take with them, and then he retreated to his home.

Tommy was playing a game when he got home, his friend Stan over with him. Jon didn't interrupt them and went straight to his room. His room had a bar, and right now, he needed a drink.

He poured himself a stiff whiskey, and sat in the lone chair, sipping it, the screen on the wall playing an old movie that he'd seen a hundred times. Soon, the prisoner would crawl through the sewer tunnel and emerge into the rain. But Jon wasn't really watching. He flinched at the bitter taste of the liquor, but he drank on it anyway, his body warming.

He should be celebrating. He had worked for years and had gotten his first taste of success. But this didn't feel like a victory. It felt like a sentence, and he didn't know why. He sent Tabby a message, asking if she was free tonight, but she didn't respond. She was probably working. At least he would have more opportunities to see her down in the dark lab.

The dark lab. He pondered those words, feeling the weight of them in his mind. He remembered the rat in his palm, its new arm treading on his skin. He had taken the rat's arm, and then he had given it back.

A knock on his door brought him back to the real world.

"Come in," he said loudly, setting down his glass, as if not holding the drink made him less tipsy.

It was Tommy, who peeked his head in before wheeling the rest of the way inside.

"Yeah?" asked Jon.

"What are we doing for dinner?" asked Tommy. "There's nothing in the fridge. Stan had to go home."

"Oh, I'm sorry," said Jon. "Just order something. Whatever you want, and I'll eat it too."

Tommy nodded, and thought to back out the door, but instead wheeled farther in.

"Are you okay, Dad?" he asked, moving closer.

"That easy to tell, huh?" asked Jon.

"Yeah," said Tommy. "You're not good at hiding things."

"Well," said Jon. "Today, we successfully had a rat regenerate a limb. We put it under, removed its arm, and with the right set of circumstances, gave him the ability to regrow it."

"Wow," said Tommy. "That's good, right?"

"Yeah," said Jon. "It is. But now me and the team are moving to the special projects lab. And I thought I'd be excited about doing that. But now—now I'm not too sure."

"Is it bad?" asked Tommy.

"I don't know," said Jon. "It's less control. And talking to Shaw—I don't know, sometimes it feels like he's threatening you, without even really trying."

Tommy looked at him, and then hugged him, reaching out to him. Jon returned it, and he attempted not to cry.

"What was that for?" asked Jon.

"I know you're doing it for me," said Tommy. "I'm sorry for yelling at you."

Jon struggled to speak and wiped away a tear. "It's not

your fault, Tommy. I'm sorry—I'm sorry for everything."

"It's okay," said Tommy. "I made a friend, at least. Have you—have you heard anything from Mom?"

"No," said Jon. "I've sent her letters."

"So have I," said Tommy. "I hope she's gotten them." He took a breath. "I miss her."

"I know you do," said Jon. "You'll see her again. I promise."

*

The next day, Jon, Stone, and their team moved into their new space. Into the special projects lab. Into the dark lab.

They wouldn't step foot back into the four pillars until it was much too late.

14

It had stunned Jon when he toured the four pillars. Each lab was expansive, with incredible equipment, with resources for hundreds of people working on cutting-edge science. It had been more to work with than he'd had in his entire career.

The dark lab dwarfed them all, combined.

Jon, Stone, Mel, and Andrew were met at the elevator doors by Sabrina again, wearing all black, her blond hair tied back in a ponytail.

"Welcome to the special project division," she said, and led them into an expansive space, segmented off into dozens of labs.

"This is incredible," said Mel. "I thought the Medical pillar was extravagant—"

"Please keep up," said Sabrina, walking at a brisk pace. "The division is much larger, and so we have more ground to cover." She wasn't lying, the corridors between labs massive, the level a labyrinth, Jon already losing track of where they entered, right after they turned once, and then twice. The glass walls were tinted black, always opaque. A few of the lab doors they passed were open, but most were closed. It was so much larger than the four pillars above. Jon struggled with the scope. Jon spied a man, dressed in all black, an assault rifle slung around his back. He stood against the wall in a corridor, looking straight ahead. He wore a tactical helmet, with a clean visor over his eyes.

"How many labs are down here?" he asked.

"A few hundred," said Sabrina. "384, counting your team."

Something didn't add up, and Jon quickly did the math in his head. There were no more than twenty teams in each pillar, which gave them only a maximum of eighty, maybe a hundred if he was being generous.

"How's that possible?" asked Jon. "There weren't that many teams to begin with."

Sabrina glanced back at him as she walked. "No one ever said that all the special projects teams had to start in one of the four pillars. Mr. Shaw moved all of his research divisions down here prior to your arrival."

Of course.

Sabrina looked forward again, and Jon tried to keep his thoughts on the present, not letting the realization of the size of Shaw's ambition distract him. He could think about what it meant later. He tried to focus and absorb all the information he was given now.

He looked through the few open doors, to see if he could glean anything, but all he saw was people, equipment, and stainless steel. They turned left at a corridor juncture, but Jon looked back the other way, and saw the glass segue into blast shielding, heavy metal, or maybe some other alloy, but it was thick, impregnable, as far as Jon could tell. More armed guards there, multiple standing in a row, dressed similarly. All black, with bulky clothing. Kevlar or flak jackets, Jon imagined.

He remembered the shielding present in the energy pillar, but this looked even tougher.

What were they testing?

But they had already left it behind. Sabrina strode with confidence.

"There are lab coats waiting for each of you in your new space," said Sabrina.

"What's wrong with these?" asked Jon.

"Nothing," said Sabrina. "But they don't have the patch."

Jon looked at a passing researcher, noticing a thick nested dark patch on his shoulder, bearing the Shaw business logo, encasing a medieval shield. Sabrina didn't explain further, and Jon didn't ask for more info.

"You'll have more resources down here," said Sabrina. Jon thought to Shaw's promise of infinite resources prior, but he guessed it must be even *more* infinite down here. A cascade of promises. "And access to more powerful tech."

"How could it more powerful than what we already had?" asked Andrew.

"I'll leave discussion around your equipment to our division manager," said Sabrina. "We're almost there."

They reached an office, but unlike the offices of the managers in the four pillars, this office was on the edge of the space, and made from the same blast shielding as Jon had seen earlier. Sabrina walked them to the door. A guard stood outside. They passed him without comment, but Jon noticed the guard's eyes on them as they entered. A man, middle-aged, with close shorn hair, dressed in a blue shirt and slacks, stood at a standing desk, six screens open in front of him. He smiled a slim smile, polite as they approached.

"This is the division manager, Dan Sherman. Mr. Sherman, this is Dr. Jon Matthews, Dr. Frank Stone, Dr. Mel Underwood, and Dr. Andrew Simmons."

"Nice to meet you all," he said. "Please, come inside."

"I'll leave them in your hands," said Sabrina, and she was gone without a goodbye.

There were no chairs in his office, so Jon didn't have to worry about sitting. Sherman closed the door behind him, a thick metal panel sliding shut with a hard SHTINK with a press of a button.

Sherman walked back around to the other side of his desk, moving the octopus of screens so they could have a clear view of each other.

"Welcome to the special projects division. I'm going to call it the dark lab, because the other thing is a mouthful. You can do the same, as long as Mr. Shaw isn't here. Shaw tells me you're regenerating limbs?"

"Yes," said Jon.

Sherman nodded. "Sounds good. Mr. Shaw told me he wants you working on chimps. How many do you need?"

"I don't know," said Jon. "We haven't worked out our plan yet."

"I'll get a dozen ready, just in case," said Sherman, matter-of-factly, and Jon's mind boggled, but he tried not to betray his confusion.

A dozen? How many animals does Shaw have down here?

"Mr. Shaw told us we'd have additional team members?" asked Jon.

"Yes," said Sherman. "I've pulled eight off of other teams through the division. Three biologists, two zoologists, two geneticists, and one surgeon, a trauma specialist. Does that sound good?"

"I—I—sure," said Jon. "That's more than what we need, I think."

"Better to overextend then to understaff, I always say," said Sherman. "If someone's just sitting around twiddling their thumbs, I can assign them to another team."

"Are they used to bouncing around?" asked Jon.

Sherman smiled, an actual smile this time. "They're our mercenaries," he said. "They go where the action is hottest. The best and brightest. You can have the highest level of confidence in them. They've already extensively studied your research, and should be able to adapt quickly. They'll work hard and fast and do what you tell them to."

They met them within ten minutes, Sherman leading them to their new lab space, extensive with a dozen workstations, its own operating theater, and walls of cages on the side of the room for holding any test subjects, before or after experimentation. Their mercenaries were already there, each sitting at their own workstation.

They gathered, each of their coats having the dark lab patch noticeable now on the shoulder.

"This is Dr. Matthews, Stone, Underwood, and Simmons. They're the project leads. Any questions?"

There were none from the eight assembled scientists. Jon wondered how long they'd been down here. They didn't look tired, or anxious, or even excited. They just looked bored.

"Good," said Sherman, after being met with silence. "Doctors, the floor is yours." Sherman left their lab without another word.

The four of them stood in front of the group, and Jon realized he should say something. He glanced at Stone and nodded to him. Stone nodded back and stepped up.

"We'll do formal introductions as we go, but Sherman told us you know the goal. Well, I'll formalize it now, straight from the mouth of god himself. We're regenerating limbs. We cut off a rat's arm yesterday, and it grew back. The next step is a chimpanzee. We want to amputate a chimp's arm and then have it grow it back. Within an hour, and on an even shorter timeline if possible. As you imagine, this is an important project to Shaw himself, and his eyes are always on us. So be ready. Go back to what you were working on, and we'll brief you individually as we devise our plans."

The eight nodded and returned to their workstations.

The four of them each set up their own, finding their new lab coats. Jon switched to his new one, running his hand over the patch on the shoulder. Such a minor distinction, but he felt it take its effect on him. He was a part of the dark lab now. A different identity.

The four of them met and decided on sub-groups within the team. They each would monitor a part, with Stone and Jon overseeing them all, and formulating a larger plan. A model was the first order of business, along with research on the chimp genome, much closer to human than the rat.

Mel pulled him aside an hour later, after she had delved

into the computer, and started the modeling process with the help of her geneticist and biologist.

"Jon, I've never seen anything like this," said Mel.

"What do you mean?" asked Jon.

"The strength of the computer," said Mel. "And that's just the tip of the iceberg. The power of the models they have here—it's just unparalleled. It doesn't seem right."

"Why not?"

"It's too advanced," said Mel. "The stuff we had in the medical pillar was state-of-the art, right on the cutting edge. This stuff is beyond that."

"Then why wouldn't Shaw just give us this stuff to begin with?" asked Jon. "If he just wanted results."

"That was my first question," she said. "He was testing us. And since we succeeded, we got the key to the kingdom. Or the key to his future tech."

Jon shook his head. "That's crazy, though."

"What else explains it?" asked Mel.

"Maybe he wanted plausible deniability," said Jon. "If we didn't make it down here. If we never progressed, we wouldn't leave with knowledge of what was down here."

Mel nodded. "Just thought I should mention it."

"You're not the only with questions," said Jon. Mel returned to work. Jon went to Stone when he saw him alone.

"Any of this strike you as weird?" asked Jon.

"All of it's weird, Jon," said Stone. "I stopped questioning it after the billionaire summoned be down to his underground science lab."

"Not that," said Jon. "The guards. The shielding. The tech. Something isn't adding up."

"Well, Shaw didn't mention he had people here prior to

the apocalypse, but it makes sense. If you have this impregnable place, why wouldn't you use it, regardless if the world was in danger or not?"

"Not even that," said Jon. "Even though the question did come up in my head. But the money here—"

"He's the world's richest man, Jon," said Stone.

"I know," said Jon. "I know. More than you and I can imagine spending in a lifetime. But Shaw says he wants to save the world. I guess I just didn't connect the dots beforehand, but it's been adding up. The cost of this place is hundreds of millions, if not billions, of dollars. Why not spend that money up top? Why not use it to save people now, instead of on research?"

"He doesn't think like that," said Stone. "He wants to change society for the better. Giving people money will feed them today, but we need to feed them for their lifetimes. And giving people money won't stop famine, or stop climate change."

"But people are suffering—"

"You have to think larger, Jon," said Stone. "That's how Shaw sees things. He's big picture. I don't agree with everything he's done, obviously, but this, I understand. He invests down here and then sees the return on a huge scale. Listen, don't think about it. It's too big for us. We should just focus on our work here. That's how we can help." Stone patted him on the back, and Jon tried to take it as reassurance, but it only felt like condescension.

Jon had come down here to realize his research, and that was happening. It would help people like Tommy and Mr. Shaw and also help others with similar problems. And nothing Stone said was wrong.

But what about those blast shields, and the armed guards? What else was going on down here? What other secrets was Shaw keeping?

15

Jon missed Tabby, and she eventually answered his messages, agreeing to see him at her place that night. Jon was exhausted from the day. After stopping by at his house to see Tommy and get dressed, he went over to Tabby's. His excitement to visit her overwhelmed his weariness.

She opened the door with a smile, but he could see the same tiredness in her motions, just a half step slower than usual. He had only been in the dark lab for a day, and it exhausted him. She'd been there for a week.

They kissed.

"I hope you don't mind macaroni and cheese," said Tabby. "I didn't have the energy to make anything else."

"That's fine with me," said Jon. "I'm not here for the food." He meant it as a joke, but Tabby didn't answer with a smart-ass comeback, which is what he expected.

"How are you doing?" he asked. Tabby had a glass of wine in front of her, already half empty, and she had just opened another bottle for him. She'd been drinking. It explained some of her slowness. Jon could see the red in her cheeks now, a dead giveaway that she'd had a few. She never slurred her words, so it was hard to tell.

"I'm alright," said Tabby, taking another sip of wine. "I'm tired."

"I can tell," said Jon. "You don't seem yourself."

"It's hard work down there," said Tabby.

"I've only been there a day," said Jon. "And I'm already exhausted. The pressure—it's real."

"You can say that again," said Tabby.

"Has it gotten any easier?" asked Jon, but Tabby didn't answer, eating another forkful of macaroni instead.

"Easier?" asked Tabby, finally.

"Yeah," said Jon. "Do you get more used to it over time?"

"Used to the dark lab?" asked Tabby.

"Yes," he said. "Do you get used to it?"

"I guess," said Tabby, avoiding eye contact. She ate more macaroni and drank another sip of wine. She wasn't rude, but she didn't want to talk about something. They finished dinner, and Jon let her have her silence. They sat down on the couch, just sitting together. Tabby had poured herself another glass of wine, even though it didn't seem to affect her, aside from her red cheeks.

Jon put his arm around her, and she leaned into him, nesting her head onto his chest. The touch felt good, and told Jon that whatever Tabby held back wasn't about him. They sat there, in silence, and Jon held her, trying to be there for her, enjoying her warmth and touch. Eventually, she spoke.

"I'm afraid to tell you what's going on."

"Why?" asked Jon.

"Because it's dangerous," said Tabby. "I think. I think you'd be in danger if I told you, and Shaw found out. And I don't want to endanger you or Tommy." She paused and took a deep breath. "I think Shaw is lying to us."

"About what?" asked Jon.

"About a lot of things," said Tabby. "But mostly, about the purpose of this place." Jon thought to the armed guards. The blast shields.

"What is the purpose, then?" asked Jon.

"I'm sorry I haven't been able to talk to you as much," said Tabby. "Or see you. I've just been so busy. We've been working eighteen-hour days for a week straight. I had to take a break tonight. My new team—they don't quit. And I'm in charge. It makes me look bad if I leave the lab before them."

"It's okay, Tabby, it really is—"

"So we've been running non-stop. And I told you that we had a working prototype of my battery design, right?"

"Yeah."

"Well, within a week, we're already past that. Two or three iterations deep. It's moving so fast. Before I've barely even looked at the thing, it's off to be tested and re-tested, with stricter and stricter requirements. How much power can we draw from it? How long is the charge cycle? Can we make it smaller? Can we make it smaller than that? Is it safe to be carried? Can we do this or that? It doesn't end." She sat up and drank more wine. "I've been drinking too much. It's the only way I can get to sleep anymore. I know it's not good sleep, but it's something, something better than nothing, which is mostly what I was getting."

Jon put his hand on her back, softly rubbing. She breathed out. "The questions they've asked about the battery. The way they talk about it. The demands they want from it. It's made me suspicious. And I try and tamp them down, but they keep coming back up. But I can't ignore my gut anymore. I think I know what they want to use my battery for."

"What's your gut say?"

Tabby turned to look at him. "That it's for a weapon."

"What kind of weapon?" asked Jon.

"That's what scares me," said Tabby. "I don't know. The power draw they need, though? It's astronomical. And they need high throughput. All the energy, all at once."

"What kind of weapon runs off a battery?" asked Jon.

"Energy weapons," said Tabby. "Plasma rifles."

"Plasma rifles?" asked Jon. "That's video game stuff. They never work in the real world."

"You're regrowing limbs, Jon," said Tabby. "I know you've only been down there a day, but Shaw has tech that I've never heard of before, either researched himself or gotten from military contractors. But the power demands they need line up with something very powerful. And it's changed the entire scope of my project. But I've gone along with it. I've made the changes they've needed, and I've only received positive feedback."

"So you're helping them?" asked Jon.

"Yeah," said Tabby. "Hence the wine. But I'm afraid not to. Because I've noticed something else. Remember Dr. Armitage?"

"Yeah," said Jon. "The saboteur. Exiled, along with his family, after setting off a fire bomb. I've seen the guards down there, with the assault rifles."

"It's not them I'm worried about," said Tabby. "At least not directly. I don't think Armitage was exiled."

"Then what?" asked Jon.

"Have you noticed anything else out of the ordinary, in the dark lab?"

Jon thought for a second. "I mean, there's a lot of weird stuff going on down there. I was caught off guard by the size of it, by the armed troops, by the amount of people that were already down there—"

"Yeah," said Tabby. "Shaw has been running this place for a longer than he's let on. Okay, I'll ask this. Did you look for any familiar faces?"

"I mean, I don't make friends like you do," said Jon. "But I kept my eyes open. I recognized a couple of people walking around, but the place is so big, it's hard to keep track."

"That's intentional," said Tabby. "It's to keep us isolated in our labs, a place that's small and familiar. So we don't get nosy."

"Well, it worked," said Jon. "I'm terrified to leave the lab."

"I forced myself out. And I walked around. No one explicitly said that I can't, and no one stopped me. I could feel the guards eyeing me, but I let them. And I didn't look at the labs. I looked at the people. I did a whole circuit."

"Jesus, that must have taken forever. The place felt gigantic."

"It's smaller than it seems. But it still took over an hour," said Tabby. "But I noticed something."

"What?" asked Jon.

"Remember when you were telling me you noticed all the people getting promoted?" asked Tabby. "You were so worried that you wouldn't make the grade."

"Yeah," said Jon. "The lab felt emptier and emptier."

"Well, theoretically, those people went down into the dark lab, right?"

"Yeah." Jon felt a sinking sensation in his gut, sensing where Tabby was headed.

"They're not there," said Tabby. "Maybe I missed them, or maybe they just stayed locked in their labs all day, but I'm pretty sure that some of those people have just disappeared."

"Is it possible there're more labs?" asked Jon. "Other facilities or levels where Shaw has put them?"

"It's possible," said Tabby. "But I don't believe it. Because my gut says that those scientists aren't in some other lab, or exiled, or transported home, to wherever that was for them. My gut says they're dead."

Jon felt his heart thump in his chest. He took a deep breath.

"If that's true, Shaw must know that someone would notice, right?" asked Jon. "He wouldn't just do it, out in the open."

"Well, there's two choices," said Tabby. "One, he didn't think anyone would notice. That with the size of this place, and the way we've shifted around, and the amount of work we do, that we would lose track of people, anyway. And some only have eyes for their work and aren't good at remembering to keep in touch. So, there's some of that, I'm sure. But everyone here is smart, and naturally curious, and incredibly skilled at critical thinking and investigation, and so I throw out choice one. If it's true, Shaw must have known that someone would notice. Or multiple someones. And that scares me too."

"Why? What's choice two?" asked Jon.

"Well, choice two is that he knows that someone would realize people are missing, and he just did it, anyway. He black bagged them, killed them, *erased* them, knowing full well the rest of the researchers down here would notice it. Whoever didn't toe the line, or he suspected of sabotage, or realized his true intentions—they disappeared. Someone like Armitage, when their impact was obvious, he made a show of it, talked about exile. But when it was someone already in the dark lab, already cut off from the rest of the researchers—they just vanish one day. Maybe even leaving an assistant or partner knowing full well what happened, but afraid to speak out."

"That's a secret police," said Jon. "Like the SS, or the KGB."

"Yes," said Tabby. "Because that's what's happening, Jon. Shaw is operating in front of us, with a smile, and handshakes, and treating us like he's a proud parent. All the while, he's taking our research and using it for whatever purpose he wants. And anyone who speaks up or out loud enough, they die. And their families die, and Shaw moves on, using their corpses as a stepping stone to the next discovery."

"Jesus fucking Christ," said Jon. He put his head in his hands. "I can't believe this."

"The signs were all there," said Tabby. "We just didn't want to believe it. But we're prisoners down here, Jon. And we have been since the moment we stepped foot inside. Sure, the jail cells are comfortable, and we can have whatever food we want. But step out of line, it's not the outside world we'll have to fear. It's an incinerator."

"I think I'll have some wine," said Jon. "Or maybe just some whiskey."

"I haven't gotten back around to Shaw's lie," said Tabby.

"What?" asked Jon. "He's lied about all of that, everything you just said."

"No, he hasn't," said Tabby. "Maybe lies of omission, if you want to count that. Which you could. But they weren't lies to our face. Because what did he tell you when you talked on the phone? When he pitched you to come down here?"

Jon remembered. Waking up to a phone call in his crappy apartment in New York.

"He told me we would save the world," said Jon.

"That's the lie," said Tabby. "A big one, one so big you wouldn't even question it. Because Shaw doesn't want to save the world, Jon. Not with all this technology, not with all this power."

Tabby downed the rest of her wine, wiping her mouth with the back of her hand.

"He doesn't want to help the world, Jon. He wants to make a new one."

16

Jon couldn't watch, not again, not seeing his failure spring up in front of him, from a living creature. Not again.

But he made himself look the entire time. If anyone was responsible, it was him, and he would bear that burden.

They had put the chimp under sedation and then removed its arm. "They" meaning his team. Jon wasn't hands on with these surgeries, only giving instructions. He had no issue. They were as good or better than he was, and he had never operated on a chimp before. He had dissected human corpses, but never a chimp.

His stomach ached as he watched them amputate the creature's arm, blood spurting out from the wound, now more than enough hands to staunch the flow of blood, to prepare the injection, to monitor the ape's vital signs.

Already, this was different from a rat. Jon had used many rats throughout his professional life. Despite his words about them toward Stone, they were disposable, more or less. Their numbers were an incredibly valuable resource, where properly bred, the number of new rats was infinite. A boon to scientists anywhere. Mice alike.

Jon had killed many rats in line with his career. He believed that you didn't waste any resource, even a nearly infinite one like rats, and he believed you didn't cause any unnecessary pain. He didn't believe in torture.

He felt a twinge of pain in his gut as they pulled the chimp from its cage and took it to the operating theater. It was one of the mercenaries, and try as he might, Jon had trouble keeping their names straight. But one of the zoologists took it from its pen, taking it to the theater, and the animal was docile, going along willingly. Jon didn't think to what its life was like up until this point.

A chimp was different. He knew all the factoids about how close humans and apes were to each other, separated so thinly along the genetic code. Jon knew that often those truths were taken too far in the zeitgeist. A lot still separated them from chimps, but Jon saw the shared heritage. Could see where humans had progressed, and chimps never had. But he recognized it, and it made his heart hurt to do it. His mind wondered how many more chimps they would operate on? What would the cost be?

But then he pushed those questions away. He could ponder them later. Any hesitation now could cost them, in results, or harm the chimp, in unnecessary suffering.

With the chimp's arm removed, they lowered it into the nutrient bath, already half filled with the white calorie-rich milk.

Another set of gloved hands and a masked face came in with the syringe, the magic serum. This was the first winner spit out by the computer model, built by the entire team, with Mel doing most of the coding. The model had given them this, and then Stone and Jon had massaged it some more, from what they had learned with the rats. It passed the eye test, but Jon knew better than to trust that.

He had expected failure, had predicted mutation and deformity, but he had still expected too much.

A minute passed, and then another, as the serum rewrote the chimp's DNA, cutting, rearranging, editing it into something different. The same as the rat, but more complex, with more systems to navigate, more side effects possible.

And then the arm regrew, bones and muscle knitting together before their very eyes. But something was wrong. The level of the nutrient bath dropped quickly, the chimp absorbing faster than they thought conceivable. The assistants stood nearby, and dumped more in, buckets full, but the creature absorbed it too quickly, and its arm mutated, becoming different, extending, growing.

"Hurry! More!" yelled Stone, through his mask, but they couldn't feed it fast enough, and its arm was barely an arm anymore, extending out of the bath, bloated muscles coated in half grown skin, with skeins of bone shooting through it, the code disrupted somewhere.

"Stop!" yelled, Jon, finally. "You're only making it worse." The assistants ceased dumping in the nutrients. "Destroy it, and then dissect it." Jon pulled off his mask, the arm finally stopping its absurd, awful growth. He walked out of the theater. Stone was right behind him.

"I don't understand—" started Stone, but Jon stopped him.

"Don't understand what?" asked Jon. "I said this would happen. Chimps are incredibly more complex animals than a rat. This sudden graduation is hopeless. We shouldn't even start with its arm. A finger to start would be much more attainable. Hell, we should take a year before we even touch a chimp—"

"Attainable is not what we're tasked with, Jon!" said Stone, his voice booming. "You know what we're after. We don't have time for baby steps, for the rigorous scientific method. We are flying on the trapeze without a safety net!"

Stone stood over him, towered over him, but then backed away. "I'll start looking over the next set of serums. We can prepare another for tomorrow."

"I can't do this every day," said Jon.

"Don't say that," said Stone. "Don't tell me you *can't* do anything. We've come this far, I don't want to hear you talk about quitting. If it takes a thousand chimps to get our results, then the cost is a thousand chimps."

"I—" started Jon, but then his phone buzzed in his pocket, and the display read Sabrina. He answered. "Hello?"

"Hello, Dr. Matthews. Sabrina Morton here. Mr. Shaw would like a word with you."

A shot of cold fear shot through Jon's heart. He remembered Tabby's words from the night before.

"I'll be right there. Should I bring Dr. Stone with me?" asked Jon. Stone's eyes narrowed at him.

"No," said Sabrina. "Just you."

"Heading down now," said Jon, and the call ended. "Shaw wants to talk to me."

Stone said nothing, only nodding. Jon left the lab, the way to the elevator still a struggle, as he weaved back and forth down unmarked corridors. He felt the guards' eyes on him as he walked, but tried to ignore it.

Worry about Shaw, not the guards. Shaw's initial meeting with them had been only days ago. What could he possibly have to say now? They'd only run one test.

Shaw didn't stand to greet Jon this time, or shake his hand with his metal prosthetic. He gestured to one of the chairs. His plasticine face didn't smile, and the great red expanse of his desk greeted Jon again.

"I hear you're struggling, Jon," said Shaw, finally, after Jon had settled in.

"I mean, we've only had a couple tests," said Jon.

"I thought you had the problem licked," said Shaw.

Jon took a deep breath. He chose his words carefully.

"Only in the rats," said Jon. "Chimps are a completely different animal, literally and figuratively."

"That's why I've given you your team, Jon," said Shaw. "Several of them have extensive experience working with and testing on chimpanzees."

"Yes, and they've been a great help," said Jon. "They've brought me up to speed on all my blind spots."

"Do you have a lot of them?" asked Shaw, and Jon felt a darkness in his tone. He didn't know if it was imagined, but he felt it.

"Blind spots?" asked Jon. "I try not to." He smiled, as genuine as he could force.

"I just want to make sure you're on the right track," said Shaw. "Obviously I have a lot invested in you and your research." He paused. "Is it true that you're seeing Dr. Knight?"

Jon smiled again, even though his face desperately resisted it. "Yes," he said. "I hope that's not a problem."

"Of course not," said Shaw, smiling his own false smile, the only he ever had. "You're both adults, and I know it does get quite lonely down here. And there are no conflicts of interest. You're on different teams. She's very smart." Is Shaw hinting at something? Does he know they talked?

You're being paranoid.

"Yes, she is," said Jon. "She stuns me, sometimes, with her intelligence."

"Can't imagine you two see each other often?" asked Shaw.

"We try and steal time when we can," said Jon. "But it is difficult. Both of us are prone to put work first."

"Well, as much as I hate to say it, that doesn't bother me," said Shaw. "How's Tommy? I've heard he's made a friend. A son of Dr. Wilson."

You hear quite a lot, you son of a bitch.

Jon smiled again, all smiles, only smiles. "Yes. He's finally settling into a routine. Obviously it's not ideal, but you know, at least he's safe down here." *Change the subject.* "Can I ask you a question, Mr. Shaw?"

"Of course," said Shaw, smiling again. "Anything."

"How is it? You know, up top?" asked Jon.

"Ah," said Shaw. "Not well. Massive food shortages and riots, across the globe. Exposure is increasing exponentially, as well. Several smaller governments have experienced coups. It's terrible. The US is surviving, but they have deployed the National Guard in multiple cities. I hope you forgive me, Jon, but it's the reason I've been so urgent. I want to deploy solutions topside as soon as possible, and I only know a foot to pedal, you know?"

Jon nodded. "Do you know how Maya is doing? My ex-wife?"

"Ah, yes," said Shaw. "Our last update has her in largely the same routine she was in prior to your arrival. She's still working. Doing her part, so to speak."

"That's good to hear," said Jon, but his mind whirled. Did he trust Shaw on even that, at this point? Or was Shaw telling him what he wanted to hear? To get his results? Jon didn't know, but he pushed it away. *Worry about him right now, you idiot.*

"I'm glad I could help," said Shaw. "If you need anything, come to me, Jon. I'm serious. Your project is number one on my plate, and if there is anything standing in your way, you tell me. I don't care what it is, we'll remove it. Understand?"

"Yes, Mr. Shaw," said Jon.

"The coming days will require sacrifice," said Shaw, standing up. "When you want to change the world, sacrifice sometimes comes right along with it. There is a strength in it. In seeing a price to be paid, and paying it gladly. I think you understand that better than most, don't you Jon?"

"I—"

"You were there when your son lost his legs, weren't you?"

CRASH, and the noise of glass shattering, of metal tearing, of calamity and disaster. They flashed through Jon's mind in an instant.

"Yes," said Jon.

"So you understand," said Shaw. "The drive, to pay down a debt. To reclaim what was taken. It's gotten you this far. Let it push you a little further. You're closer to your goal,

Jon. We can reach it, together. Just push harder."

"Yes, Mr. Shaw," said Jon, again. He just wanted out of here. He couldn't breathe. His heart thudded like machine gun fire inside his chest.

"Good to hear," he said, walking over and extending his hand again. Jon stood and shook it, and its grip was tight, squeezing harder than before. Or was that only in Jon's imagination?

"Push yourself and your team, Jon, and you'll find your success," said Shaw. "There is no room for stagnation in the special projects division. And there is no tolerance for anything but success."

Jon nodded this time, ready and waiting for the metal prosthetic to let him go, to get out of the grip of Shaw, get out of this office, back to the elevator, and he did, and then as the doors closed, he stood there gasping.

A few minutes later, he asked Nadia for travel back to the dark lab, and she complied wordlessly. He looked to the camera in the ceiling. Was she watching him, as he panted away the panic that had risen in his guts?

Was Shaw?

17

The pressure didn't ease on Jon or his team. It only built as more and more failure piled up.

Jon looked away from another mutated chimpanzee, its arm distended and horrible, twice as long as the other limbs, massive, with bulging muscle breaking through the skin, the bone punching through both. Luckily, the chimp would never awaken again.

Jon threw his mask in the bin with disgust and walked out of the operating theater, leaving his team to clean up the mess. It was late, but Jon didn't really know what day it was anymore. There was nothing that separated them, only periods of work and sleep, with brief interruptions for necessary bodily functions.

He thought he had seen Tommy this morning, but he

couldn't remember now. He wiped his eyes, thinking there was something in them, but they were just bleary. He was exhausted, the whole team was exhausted. You could see it in the way they moved. It had been two weeks since his talk with Shaw, and they had gotten nowhere. They had tried, and tried some more, but nothing.

Stone walked out shortly behind him, and Stone, normally indefatigable, also drooped, his feet scraping along the tile floor.

"I need a drink," said Stone.

"We need to do another tonight," said Jon.

"Why?" asked Stone. "It's not like we're getting anywhere."

"We have to keep pushing," said Jon. "We need results to work with if we're going to adjust the model."

"You sound like me, Jon," said Stone, wearily. "Okay. One more tonight. But I don't have much hope. We've already gone through the most promising serums."

Stone retreated to his workstation, to prepare for one more procedure.

Jon thought over Stone's words. He did sound like him, but he had been left with little choice. He felt the pressure hanging over all of them, a sword of Damocles ready to swing at the next failure. And that same pressure had pushed away his hesitance and anxiety about experimenting on the chimps. He had become desensitized, after an endless parade of animals had been brought up into the lab, ready for Jon to perform his mad science on. One by one, they had been put under, had their arm amputated, and then would deform, mutate, and be destroyed and dissected. Jon watched each time, making himself bear the burden of such terrible atrocity. It was his doing, he should at least own that. But he wasn't alone.

The rest of the team watched as well, even Mel, who had cared so much about the rats. She still flinched but she had hardened in her time down here. Just like he had. Normally he would have dismissed his team hours ago, but Shaw wanted results, and his conversation with Tabby hadn't left his mind in any waking moment. Had Shaw killed those who disagreed with him? Or couldn't meet his expectations?

Jon didn't know, but he didn't want to test him. He wanted to see his research bear fruit, but there was more there now. Now survival was at stake, and more importantly, Tommy's survival. Jon didn't know what would happen to Tommy if Jon was exiled or killed, but he doubted it would be good. Shaw, for all of his magnanimity and desire to do good, only wanted people who would serve his purposes. No hangers on. No leeches. No parasites.

How long had they been down here? Only a couple months, but time had lost all meaning. He remembered wanting to find the answers to his research, to help Tommy. Now he only wanted Tommy to survive.

And Jon would need to get results to guarantee it.

Mel approached him.

"Jon—"

"Tell the team to get another chimp ready," said Jon. "We need to do another tonight."

"I don't think—"

"Don't question me," said Jon, his voice hard, and Mel averted her eyes and retreated. Jon felt a pang of guilt, but pushed it away. It was for the best. They needed results.

With the last chimp euthanized, and one of the biologists already working on an autopsy, they prepared for another procedure. It was clockwork now, with all the players knowing their roles, even if they tired of them, tired of killing animals for no real progress.

They moved, doing their pieces. Sedating the animal. Removing the arm. The nutrient bath. The new serum. Standing by with more nutrients.

Jon stared at it, studying each part, trying to parse where the failure lied. They had gotten more and more information with each chimp, but no closer to success. They had fine tuned the serum, accelerating and decelerating the regeneration, the absorption, the rate of change, the transfer of cell growth, but none of it had proven any more successful. It felt like a crap shoot, directionless, and Jon hated it. But the only way out was through.

"Injecting the serum," said Steven, one of the biologists, and the chimp regrew the arm. They had slowed down the growth again with this mixture, hoping that the chimp's healing wouldn't outpace the absorption rate, that it would be slower but wouldn't spur an extraneous rate of deformity.

Jon watched as the arm slowly regrew. He held his breath, waiting for success. They needed it now. They couldn't afford any more time. He imagined Shaw watching through a camera, sitting behind his clean red desk, his metal prosthetic fingers noiselessly moving as he waited.

The bone re-knit, and the assistants poured more nutrients in, keeping the chimp awash in fuel. Its new skin absorbed the calories. They had transformed it into an engine, delivering cells to the wound site.

Jon held his breath. This was the moment. He felt it. Minutes passed, and the arm grew before his eyes. His heart had caught in his throat, unable to breathe, a wave of relief ready to break and wash through him. They would succeed, they would survive, Tommy *would* walk again—

No.

The arm started mutating again, and Jon couldn't watch anymore, couldn't stomach anymore failure, and he left, pushing hard through the theater doors, back into the main lab, throwing anything he could find.

"Goddamnit!" he yelled, turning over equipment carts, metal clanking against the ground, beakers shattering.

"Get a hold of yourself," said Stone, coming up behind him.

Jon wheeled to face him. "Leave me alone."

"Really?" asked Stone. "You push us toward another experiment, another failed experiment, and now you want to be left alone. Don't give me that."

"Fuck off, Stone," said Jon, his temper flaring, words swallowed a hundred times now voiced.

"Very professional," said Stone. The rest of the team stood on the edge of the doorway, looking in, watching as the two of them argued. "Do you think you're the only one struggling?"

"I—"

"We're all feeling the pressure," said Stone. "But no one else is throwing things. No one else is swearing. You're the one losing control, right when we need you the most."

Jon felt another pang of guilt, but it was swallowed up by his anger.

"You don't understand—"

"I understand perfectly well," said Stone. "I know that for two weeks we've been grinding ourselves to the bone, doing things your way, and we've gotten nothing but failure. You meet with Shaw privately, say nothing about the meeting, and then cry when things don't work out. Why are you even here?"

"What?" asked Jon. "Are you—"

"Why are you on the team, Jon?" asked Stone. "Do we need you at all? You're dragging us all down. I told you we needed to push the chimps harder, and you dismissed the thought out of hand—"

"This is my research!" said Jon. "You'd still be in the medical pillar if it wasn't for me!"

"Excuse me?" asked Stone. "Without my help, you and your boy would be out in the cold, where you belong!"

Jon leapt at Stone then, swinging with a fist and missing, Stone dodging the blow. Stone grabbed Jon with a thick arm and punched him with the other, smashing Jon in the nose and then eye, and stars sprang into Jon's vision with bright sparks of pain. Jon swung once more and connected with a lucky strike, his knuckles opening up Stone's eyebrow.

Then the rest of the team swarmed them, pulling them apart, both panting, red-faced, and angry. Blood trickled from Jon's nose. Stone surged against the sea of bodies and arms holding him back, trying to get to Jon again, but they held firm, and he stopped, breathing hard.

"Jon," said Mel, standing to the side, holding her phone. Jon stared at her, confused.

"Shaw wants you both in his office," said Mel. "Now."

Panic and fear surged into Jon's heart, replacing his rage. He had been all instinct and anger, buried inside for months now, but it all vanished in an instant. He looked to Stone, who met his eyes with the same terror. Despite their argument, they both shared it.

The assistants gradually let go of both of them. Jon straightened his lab coat and grabbed a tissue to hold to his nose. Stone did the same for his eyebrow, and then they left the lab, walking to the elevator, one after the other.

They said nothing as the elevator sped them to Shaw's office. Both still panted, trying to catch their breath.

Shaw waited for them in his office, standing, his back to them.

"Don't sit," said Shaw, without turning. "This won't take long."

The sudden fear and terror in Jon's heart doubled then, tripled, his mind immediately rotating through the terrible things that awaited them, awaited Tommy. They had failed; they had embarrassed themselves, they would—

"Are you both children?" asked Shaw, turning back toward them. Despite the lateness of the hour, he looked no different that he ever did. Jon had always heard about his incredibly long hours, his routine nights of only four hours sleep. If he was tired, he didn't show it.

Neither answered, not knowing what to say.

"Squabbling in front of your team?" asked Shaw. "Pointing fingers? Shameful. I bring you both down here, give you the world to work with. Give you both enough to realize your dreams, and you are letting it slip through your fingers!"

Jon realized he'd never heard Shaw yell, but now his staid face was curled in anger, spittle flying from his lips, onto his clean, red desk.

"You work, day after day, and come up with nothing but failure, and then, because that wasn't enough, you fight amongst yourselves, like children, like idiots! We are the best and brightest in the entire world, and still, we resort to a fistfight like common thugs! It's embarrassing, disappointing."

Shaw panted now, out of breath after yelling.

"Do you think this is acceptable?" he asked, finally. He waited.

"No," said Jon, with Stone echoing him a few seconds later.

"Good," said Shaw. "You still have a modicum of sense, somewhere in those brains of yours. Because none of this is acceptable. I expect success. These endless failures will not stand. And this infighting will stop now. If this happens again, both of you are gone. Understood?"

"Yes," said Jon and Stone, almost together.

"Good," said Shaw. "Go home. Sleep. But tomorrow, I want results. No more damaged chimps. No more fighting. I want success. We are running out of time, gentleman. The world is eating itself above our heads. Get results, or you will be the next course."

18

"We have to push it harder."

Jon and Stone sat across from each other. They were in the lab early, before any of the rest of the team. Jon's nose ached, and he sported a black eye. Stone's eyebrow had scabbed over, but he would keep a nasty scar, even after it healed.

"We can't," said Jon. "It won't be able to take it. It's too much change, too quickly."

"How do you know that?" asked Stone.

"Every time I've tried to institute too many changes at once, there's massive large scale cellular disruption," said Jon. "The animal's DNA is overloaded with revisions, especially in such a short amount of time. It melts down, at a cellular level. It's—it's awful to look at. I can't imagine what the animal feels."

"But slowing it down hasn't worked," said Stone. "We still get mutation and deformity. With the rats, speeding them up was the only thing that worked. Matching their absorption rate of nutrients to the regeneration was the thing that staved off the mutations."

"The chimp's arm is larger," said Jon. "That's what I don't get. We've pushed its absorption rate as hard as we can. They absorb the nutrient bath so quickly. How many gallons did we go through on the last chimp?"

"Two dozen," said Stone.

"So it's not that," said Jon. "It can't be. Hell, we're doubling what the scale model says, and it's still burning through it. We're only supercharging the anomaly."

"So, why is the mutation still occurring, even though we've exceeded the necessary absorption rate?" asked Stone.

Jon thought back to the rat, of it scurrying on his arm after it had regenerated. That success had felt like the key to everything, but it hadn't given them enough to go on with the chimps. Shaw had forced them to take a massive leap forward, and they couldn't cover the gap. Jon absentmindedly scribbled on a notepad.

"Could it be the immune system overreacting?" asked Jon.

"We already suppress it as much as we can," said Stone. "It's effectively off while the wound heals, but it shouldn't be a problem. Nothing we're giving them should trigger it."

"Goddamnit," said Jon. "A chimp is ten times more complicated than a rat. And a human is even worse. Shaw—"

"Don't," said Stone, softly. An unspoken threat was there, underneath that word, but not a threat from Stone, but the menace that hung over both of them.

"I don't know what to do," said Jon.

"I'm telling you, we have to push it harder," said Stone. "Push the absorption rate even harder. The mutation happens because there's not enough fuel and the regenerative cells lose cohesion."

"It'll burn itself out," said Jon. "It's too much. Even with its skin—wait—I've got it. You're right."

"What?" asked Stone. "Say it again. It sounds good."

"I mean, not directly," said Jon. "But you're right. We need to push it harder. But not in the same place. What if, instead of increasing the absorption rate, we increased the bandwidth of the consumption?"

"You mean, broadening the skin's tolerance level?" asked Stone. He pondered it over for a moment. "I've never tried that before."

"It *would* effectively increase the rate of absorption," said Jon. "But there'd be less delay. That might be the problem. On a micro level, and on a larger scale, it could be costing us."

"That actually makes sense," said Stone. "We'll have to try it. But it could lead to unpleasant side effects. The skin quality afterward could suffer as well—"

"We'll have to cross that bridge when we come to it," said Jon. "Can we code this into a model with enough time?"

"I doubt it," said Stone. "Even if Mel busted her ass, we wouldn't get results before the end of the day. Tomorrow, at the earliest."

"We could always ask Shaw for an extension," said Jon.

"I don't think he's in the mood for that," said Stone. "Even if it is reasonable."

"Then we'll eyeball it," said Jon. "Using our best guess and the computer to build it."

"It's worth a shot," said Stone. "But my confidence isn't exactly high. There's so much that could go wrong."

"PMA," said Jon. "PMA."

"PMA?" asked Stone. "What does that mean?"

"Positive mental attitude," said Jon. "My ex used to tell me whenever I got gloomy. Be positive, and good things will follow."

"I've always been more of a follower of Murphy's law," said Stone.

They worked, and soon the rest of the team arrived, fresher and smarter than the night before. Jon and Stone delegated tasks among the team, but still the brunt of the workload fell on them. They didn't go it entirely alone. Mel wrangled the computer into giving them an assist, not as good as a full-on model, but better than nothing.

Half-way through the day they had a serum. The CRIS-PR software gave it a pass with some quick simulations, but results on an actual chimp hadn't matched the models yet.

"I think this is it," said Jon. "We're running out of time."

"Let's not stand on ceremony," said Stone. "Let's start the show."

Shaw wanted results. Well, they'd get them today, good or bad. It was in the spirit of the FUTURE lab. Everything riding on an unproven theory and going by gut instinct. Jon and Stone hadn't told the rest of the team what Shaw had told them, but they still worked on pins and needles. Would Shaw actually follow through if they didn't make any progress today? Jon didn't know, but it didn't stop his heart from threatening to pound its way through his chest.

They prepped the chimp as always, everything falling into their typical rhythm. They all gathered around, ready to step in if needed. Gallon after gallon of the nutrient bath was ready to dump into the container, more than they could ever need.

If we even get there. Jon's biggest fear was the serum killing the ape outright. Cellular death, its DNA unraveling in front of their very eyes. A few tweaks to the serum is all it would take, and they did more than just tweak it.

The chimp was sedated now, its body limp, its breath shallow, an oxygen mask covering its mouth. The zoologist moved in, ready to take off its arm. Jon hoped this wouldn't be the last time it would have it.

They worked quickly, expertly, amputating the arm, all the while keeping blood loss to a minimum. They moved in and transported the animal to the nutrient bath. It was time for the moment of truth. Stone moved in with the serum, doing it himself. Jon watched as he injected it into the chimp. Jon's heart thudded in his chest, a hollow ache in his gut burning hot.

They all watched with bated breath. Several assistants waited with more of the nutrient bath, heavy containers full of the milky white substance. The arm began to regrow. The bone first, forming from the shoulder, a clean cut, something they'd almost never have in real life. It grew, knitting before their eyes. The chimp absorbed the nutrient bath even faster now, its skin a sieve, the liquid pouring through it. They refilled it quickly, keeping the bath full, even as more and more of it went into the animal.

Its arm continued to regrow. As the bone extended out to the elbow, the muscle covered it. Red, viscous tissue grew, thin at first, and then thicker, multiple layers piled together, the incredible strength of the animal lying within.

Minutes had passed, and Jon couldn't take his eyes off the animal. None of them could. They knew what was riding on it. Time both sped and crawled, Jon anxious for results but also dreading failure.

An elbow grew then, a knot of bone, a hinge, and the forearm sprung from it. Muscle trailed behind it, cartilage knitting in the elbow in front of it. Back near the wound site, skin formed, layer by layer.

Jon's heart thumped, as hard as it ever had, the same feeling he had when Tommy was being born, of waiting on a result he had no control over, not anymore.

The bone continued to regenerate, the nutrient bath being depleted as fast as ever. Ulna and radius formed, two separate bones in the forearm. Jon watched, waiting, dreading that any moment the bones and muscle and skin would balloon, would distort, would mutate into something else, something unrecognizable as animal or man, as flesh grown unbound.

He waited, and the arm continued to regenerate. Hair grew on the skin on the shoulder, finishing there, spreading slowly behind the growth of the skin. The twin bones of the forearm met at the wrist. Another complicated hinge. A broken wrist and a chimp would die in the wild, unable to survive without a working hand.

But the wrist formed next, bone first, and then cartilage on top, working out toward the palm and fingers.

Almost there, almost there. Jon felt his fingernails cut into his palms. He made himself relent before he bled.

The finger bones stopped forming, done, and they

watched, minute by minute, as the muscle filled in behind it. Behind that, the skin, and the hair.

Jon's breath came a little bit easier, and he smiled behind his surgical mask, unable to stop himself.

And then the chimp's arm was there, whole again, no different from the one it had replaced. It's skin, the main worry voiced by Stone, looked fine. It had a little of a sheen on it, like the chimp had just gotten out of the shower, but was otherwise whole.

Someone whooped, and others yelled in celebration.

"Don't celebrate yet," said Jon. "Prepare to revive. And get the killshot ready."

A rat, once revived, can only do so much damage. A chimp, on the other hand, even one that is normally docile, can wreak havoc, especially if it's in pain, or afraid. The killshot was a syringe with a potent chemical cocktail that would functionally destroy its central nervous system.

The team put aside the nutrient bath and picked the chimp out of its tub, moving it back to the main operating table. They toweled it off as they ceased the sedative. Soon it moved, its breath coming more and more normal. Jon watched it carefully. Would its arm still work? Its vitals were stable, but things could fall apart in a moment. They waited, all watching the animal.

Its eyes blinked open, groggy at first, looking around slowly. They waited, giving it time for the sedative to wear off. Its arm twitched, and it reflexively reached around for purchase. With both its arms.

More time passed, minute by minute, and the chimp recovered fully. It vocalized, and then the zoologist picked it up, and held it, just as he had cradled it as he brought it to the table. The creature wrapped its arm around him.

"Now we can celebrate," said Jon, smiling. The team yelled and cheered.

"I don't know how that worked," said Stone. "It was a one in a million shot."

"It's almost like we're good at this," said Jon. "Well, we got results. How long until Shaw requests a meeting?"

Stone pulled his phone from his pocket. Sabrina was already calling.

19

Shaw was all smiles now, standing, greeting them not with handshakes, but with hugs, wrapping his arms around them with glee.

"I knew you boys could do it," he said. "I knew a little fire underneath would get you going, and my god. I watched the whole thing. It's incredible. Seeing it in a rat is one thing, but in a chimp? Unbelievable." The fingers of his metal arm moved back and forth, back and forth, and Jon had to force himself not to watch it. "Sit down. Let's talk about what's next."

Jon and Stone sat down, seats now familiar again, welcomed back into Shaw's good graces, just like that. Jon breathed easier, but even so, it was hard for him to sit comfortably. He remembered Shaw's screaming at them, spittle flying everywhere. He remembered Armitage. He remembered Tabby's conjecture. Had Shaw heard that too?

They had all been told that there were no cameras in personal living spaces, but their phones and tablets all had cameras and microphones installed. Jon had initially trusted that they weren't spying on him, but he wasn't sure now.

"So, what's next?" asked Shaw, his hands open.

"Well," said Jon. "I would suggest we work at optimizing the serum we have on chimps. Getting it to perform better, and making sure it's safe, long term. And then we can transition to human testing, but carefully. Humans are not rats, or chimps—"

"Yes, yes," said Shaw. "Human lives are much more precious. But better—what do you mean by better?"

"More efficient," said Jon. "I'm sure Dr. Stone and I can fine tune the sequencing, and optimize certain processes."

"Will that make it faster?" asked Shaw.

"It might," said Jon. "Incrementally, but it wouldn't be the main goal. We're already under an hour—"

"It's a good start," said Shaw. "But I want more. Faster. More damage."

"We've already got a chimp regenerating a limb in under an hour," said Jon. "That, in and of itself, is a minor miracle."

Shaw paused, considering him. He smiled, finally.

"Limb regeneration is just the start, Jon," said Shaw. "I know, I know. You look at me, and you see this." He raised his prosthetic. "We talked about it on your first day here. Because what is this?"

"It's rope," said Jon.

"I'm glad you remember," said Shaw, smiling widely. "This is rope. But this isn't the extent of it. Think about the human body, and all the things we do to it to compensate for its weakness. Prosthetic limbs. Organ transplants. Blood transfusions. All of them, rope. They are humanity doing their best with simple tools. Truly, it is why we were able to climb out of the muck, and dominate the Earth. But I am not satisfied with simply replacing my arm, Jon. Do I want a new arm? Of course. This accursed thing is the most valuable thing in the world, but I would kill to write with my own hand again." He moved his prosthetic, tapping on the table. *Tink tink tink.*

"But making this incredible piece of technology obsolete is only the beginning," said Shaw. "It is a proof of concept. Because I don't want to just replace my arm, or your son's legs. I want to eliminate trauma all together. No more bullet wounds. No more damage from shrapnel. No more reconstructed knees or shoulders. Catastrophic car accidents, plane crashes, even things like falling off a ladder. No more lasting effects. No more lingering injuries. Imagine, a world where a father falls off a roof and breaks his back. Normally, the man would be burdened with that damage for the rest of his life. He would carry that trauma until he died. And that is after years of rehabilitation and pain management. No more. We erase it, the broken bones re-stitching themselves back together."

Shaw stood up now, pacing behind his desk.

"Imagine, a soldier, blown to pieces by an IED. A simple soldier, out on patrol, and his legs are destroyed. He surrenders his mobility for the rest of his life, loses his identity, his sense of self, his agency over his body. The armed forces lose a soldier, wastes a resource. But instead of that damage, he heals. His limbs regrow on the field, a single medic overseeing the procedure."

Shaw stared at Jon, now.

"Imagine, Jon. A boy, in a car accident. A semi-truck, tears through the car he's driving in, removing his legs in an instant. Imagine, instead of a lifetime in a wheelchair, he regrows them, in a few minutes. Imagine, trauma. Instead of a lifetime of hardship, it instead, is a momentary struggle, immediately overcome."

"You have a proof of concept," said Shaw. "And frankly, you've already done the hardest work. That is why I ask for more. Because right now, we are almost there. We are on the brink. You just need to take the final step. Should damage to another part of the body be any different from regenerating a limb?"

Jon looked to Stone, who only stared back at him blankly. "I—I don't know," said Jon. "Theoretically, no. But in practice, who can say? Everything gets more complex when you introduce test subjects, with an infinite amount of variables thrown in."

"But it should work?" asked Shaw.

Jon took a deep breath. "I would think so."

"Good," said Shaw. "Because I ask for one other thing."

Jesus Christ, what more could he want?

"Yes?" asked Jon.

"I want live testing," said Shaw.

"Live testing?" asked Jon. "You mean, do the experiments on conscious animals?"

"Yes," said Shaw. "Humans in the field will be conscious, when they regenerate. So we must test on conscious animals."

"I—I don't know we can feasibly implement live testing,"

said Jon. "Removing a limb from a conscious animal, doing any other trauma—It's unconscionable. It's torture."

"Let me ask you a question, Jon," said Shaw, his smile disappearing. "How many chimps would you kill to give your son his legs back?"

"I—"

"It's more than one, or two. How many have you killed so far? Sure, they've been sedated, so their pain was minimal. How many would you maim? How many would you deal trauma to, to erase your son's?"

Jon stared at him, his breath catching in his lungs. He thought to the scene of the accident, of Tommy lying there, blood pouring out of his legs.

"I don't know," said Jon, finally.

"Well, you need to find an answer," said Shaw. "Because I have mine. I would kill as many as it takes. March them in here, one by one. I would mow them down with machine gun fire, over and over again. Chop through them with a machete, until they piled in my office. Until the floor was thick with their blood. I would kill them until I drowned, if it meant by arm back." He stared at Jon, his plastic face determined, his eyes hollow. "This is an end to trauma, Jon. An end to conflict. When all soldiers are invincible, war becomes impossible. The pain of a chimp is not among my concerns. Do you understand?"

"Yes," said Jon.

"As for implementing testing," said Shaw. "You two are bright, as is everyone on your team. Find solutions. You've done splendidly so far at that. Your work is getting closer and closer to real life implementation. Every step you take is one closer to solutions in the real world. And not a moment too soon. There was a nuclear blast, on the surface."

"What?" asked Jon.

"Where?" asked Stone.

"Moscow," said Shaw. "Sent by Pakistan. There have been small conflicts for weeks, and Putin thought that he could bluff them by cutting off their last supply chain. He thought wrong."

"Holy hell," said Jon, trying to catch his breath. "How many dead?"

"They're still counting," said Shaw. "Millions. Putin himself, they're not sure. He might have escaped. The news is still coming in. But now everyone waits for Russian reprisal."

"Fuck," said Stone.

"So you see, we must act quickly," said Shaw. "Multiple other teams are nearly complete. You are catching up, which I applaud. But believe me, my insistence is not for selfish reasons. We must intervene before the world ends. We must introduce ourselves while something still remains."

Jon's mind boggled at the thought of nuclear war. He had always dismissed the idea, even as more and more countries armed themselves. The threat of mutual destruction always felt too dangerous for even the most deranged ruler to pull the trigger. He couldn't fathom the amount of life lost.

"Do you understand, now?" asked Shaw, again.

They both nodded, solemnly.

Jon's heart hurt, and the thought of inflicting trauma on live test subjects made his stomach ache, and bile rise into his throat. But Shaw wasn't wrong. If they could broaden the use of the serum to eliminate trauma all together, it would revolutionize the world. It would change everything.

"Good luck, gentlemen," said Shaw, and they left. The team still celebrated upon their return. Neither Jon or Stone had the heart to tell them about the attack on Moscow. It didn't matter, as the news hit the Shawnet minutes later, and that was all anyone talked about.

Jon and Stone secluded themselves, and drew up plans about how to institute live testing. The amount of variables increased exponentially, and not only increased pain to the animal, but increased the danger to the researchers. A creature in pain or distress was dangerous, and a chimp even more so. They could injure or kill any member of the team if there weren't multiple levels of safeguards and protocol in place. Jon and Stone dismissed the rest of the team for the day, letting them go home and deal with the news.

Jon and Stone worked for hours, coming up with some preliminary ideas for live testing. They would bounce it off the team the next day. Stone would talk to Sherman and get some armed guards. They would need a different testing area. The theater wouldn't get it done. They needed something stronger. Something bulletproof.

The aching pit in Jon's stomach didn't go away as they drew up plans. It only got worse and worse, getting so bad Jon had to excuse himself, running to the bathroom to throw up bile into the sink. He tried to drink water, but nothing made the pain go away. Because despite everything, despite the promise of healing Tommy, despite the nuclear attack and the urgency it created, he still didn't think he could hurt the animals like they would require. This wasn't rats, and they weren't sedated. He didn't know how the rest of the team would react either.

Shaw's demands had only increased with time, and Jon's

mind worried about what he would ask for next. And Jon, when he had sat next to Stone in Shaw's office, had thought to just say no. Because there were lines he simply wouldn't cross.

But after his conversation with Tabby, he had went for walks as well. And he noticed just how empty the FUTURE lab actually was. There was still many people down there, but for the size of it, it was largely uninhabited. But it hadn't been that way just two weeks prior. People were missing.

Where had they gone? Were they back in the four pillars? Were they in their rooms, resting, having reached the end of their research, having realized the fruit of their labor?

Or were they exiled? Sent back to the surface without help or lifeline?

Were they dead?

Hours passed, and Stone left him alone in the lab. They had done all the work they could do today, both exhausted from the work and from the news of the attack.

Jon sat alone. His phone buzzed. It was a text from Tabby. They had only briefly talked over the last few days, sending fleeting text messages, and one brief phone conversation before bed.

We need to talk sent Tabby.

When? Jon replied.

Tonight. Now.

About what? Jon asked in a reply, but she never answered. Jon waited on a response, but then packed up his things and went home. He talked to Tommy briefly, still waiting on a reply. It never came. Tabby always responded quickly to his texts. This wasn't like her.

After saying goodbye to Tommy, he realized why Tabby

hadn't answered.

She didn't want it on the Shawnet.

20

Tabby hugged him hard, squeezing him tightly as soon he opened the door. He returned it. He needed it, frankly. She whispered in his ear.

"Don't say anything," she said. "Give me your phone."

She let go of him and he pulled his Shaw phone out of his pocket, handing it to her. She wordlessly took it into her bedroom. She returned a moment later, closing the door behind her.

"I don't know if it matters, honestly," said Tabby. "But I might as well."

"You think they're listening?" asked Jon.

"Yes," said Tabby, quickly. "Actively? I don't know. You'd have to have a lot of people on staff to listen to every device's microphone around the clock. But maybe Shaw is crazy enough to do it."

"I mean, if he really wanted, he could hide microphones and cameras in all the living spaces," said Jon.

"I looked," said Tabby. "Pretty extensively. Nothing that I could recognize as one. That doesn't mean they're not here, but I find it doubtful."

"Won't they find it suspicious that you're hiding the phones and tablets in the house?" asked Jon.

"I'd rather them be suspicious and not know what we're saying," said Tabby. "I'm sorry. For all of this."

"It's not your fault," said Jon.

"I know," said Tabby. "I just wish—I wish I had met you anywhere else."

"At least we're safe down here," said Jon. "Jesus Christ. Maybe I'm naïve, but I really didn't think anyone would resort to nuclear weapons. God, Moscow. There has to be millions dead. And there will be more in Pakistan, probably exponentially more. There won't be a Pakistan left—"

"Jon, there was no nuclear attack," said Tabby.

"What?" asked Jon. "Have you not seen the news on Shawnet? God, the pictures—"

"It's a lie, Jon," said Tabby, her voice dry, and calm. "There was no attack."

"How do you know that?" asked Jon. "Hell, Shaw told me himself—"

"That clinches it," said Tabby. "There was no attack. Pakistan wouldn't bomb Moscow."

"Why not?" asked Jon. "I mean, I didn't want to believe it, but it sounds plausible. From what I know, there's some simmering resentment there—"

"Resentment, yes," said Tabby. "But nothing to trigger

nuclear war. And especially not over supply lines. Please. Pakistan is having the same trouble everyone is, but why would they target Moscow? Russia would wipe them off the map, and no matter how bad the casualties were, Russia is far too big to do any significant damage. You'd have to do dozens of strikes, which Pakistan doesn't have the capability or will for."

"Again, how do you know that?" asked Jon.

"My ex worked in the state department," said Tabby. "Pakistan was one of his assignments. Believe me, I've heard more about Pakistani government and culture than I would want in ten lifetimes. But the way he talked about it, the Pakistanis would sooner eat their own tail than attack Russia, via conventional or nuclear war."

"We've been down here for a while," said Jon. "Maybe things changed."

"That's possible," said Tabby. "But I don't believe it, not for a second. I'm sure Shaw chose those two countries because he didn't think anyone would question it. But after everything else he's done, I don't believe that it happened. Moscow is fine. I mean, they're probably not *fine*, but they're not nuked."

Tabby's face displayed only confidence.

"So another lie?" asked Jon. "But why?"

"Why any of the lies?" asked Tabby. "To help control us. To inspire fear and obedience. What did you feel when he told you?"

Jon paused. "Overwhelming sorrow," said Jon. "I was just awash in it."

"When did he tell you?" asked Tabby.

"Jesus, I forgot to tell you!" said Jon. "We were successful! A chimp regenerated an arm!"

"Congrats," said Tabby. "Good work." Her eyes showed something else, though.

"What's wrong?" asked Jon.

Tabby looked away from him and then back. "I'm glad you've finally done it, Jon. But it only makes me more scared. Is that when he told you?"

"We had a meeting to discuss what's next," said Jon. "And he wants us to push the animals harder. Try and expand our results, so we can regenerate all trauma, in more varied situations. He told us to go to live testing."

"On live chimps?" asked Tabby. "And all trauma?"

"Yes," said Jon. "He mentioned all kinds of things. Car accidents, household mishaps, soldiers—"

"He mentioned soldiers?" asked Tabby.

"Yeah," said Jon. "He said that it's within our grasp to end combat trauma. Soldiers would just heal bullet and shrapnel wounds, quickly. There'd be no more amputees, or anyone hurt, at all."

"Fucking hell," said Tabby, and she got up now, and paced in the living room, staring at the floor.

"I knew it, I knew it," said Tabby. "Jesus fucking Christ, I knew it, and I helped them anyway. Fuck!"

Jon stared at her. "What's wrong?"

She stopped and breathed. "Sorry. Finish. Please. When did he tell you?"

"He told me at the end of the meeting," said Jon. "I was—I wouldn't say arguing with him, but I was certainly not happy with the idea of using live subjects. He tried to convince me with a really long spiel, and then told us at the end about the attack. Said we all need to hurry, because the world is ending, and we need to stop it."

Tabby sat down next to him again. She squeezed his hand and started shaking, and Jon realized she was crying. He grabbed and held her. He held her until she stopped, reaching for a tissue and wiping away her tears.

"It's my fault," she said, finally. "It's my fault."

"What's wrong?" asked Jon. "What's your fault?"

"They showed me the weapon, Jon," said Tabby. "They showed me what my battery is powering. I saw it work, for the first time."

"What is it?" asked Jon.

"It shouldn't exist," said Tabby. "It's some sort of plasma beam weapon. As a work of engineering, it's nothing short of remarkable. I don't know how it works, and I was afraid to ask. But my battery powers it. It wouldn't work without—"

She cried again, but stopped herself, grabbing another tissue.

"It has phenomenal power demands," said Tabby. "Even my battery can only give it a few charges. At least right now. But even one charge, my god, it's power."

"They showed you?" asked Jon, trying to focus her.

"Yeah," said Tabby. "I guess they bought my playing along, because they were excited to show me it. Shaw had already seen a demonstration, but their lead thought I deserved one as well. Considering how instrumental I was. It's no bigger than a normal rifle. But it has no bullets. It has internal laser and gas systems, but I didn't see any of that. I only saw the damage it did."

"What can it do?"

"I saw them test it on a cow," said Tabby, swallowing. "A live one."

"Christ," said Jon. "Where are they keeping all these animals?"

"I assume there's an animal habitation level, somewhere in here," said Tabby. "But it was a cow. Docile. And we all wore dark goggles, like the kind you wear to look at the eclipse. Or for welders. We wore goggles, and they plugged in my battery, and the rifle charged. It was silent, almost completely. The only noise it makes is when it fires, and it's just a really loud click. No louder than someone snapping their fingers. It clicks, and an incredibly bright light flashed. It hurt my eyes, even behind the goggles, and I blinked, because I wasn't expecting it, and when I could see again, the cow was gone. Only—only parts were left."

"At least it didn't suffer," said Jon.

"They told me the range on it, Jon," said Tabby. "It has a range of miles. No drop off. No way to disrupt it. Pair it with a targeting system, and—"

"And say goodbye," said Jon.

"It obliterates flesh, and metal, and brick, and stone, and anything else," said Tabby. "And I helped power it."

"You didn't have a choice," said Jon. "More people are missing. I don't know what Shaw is doing with them, but it can't be good."

"There's always a choice," said Tabby. "It just wasn't a good one. It doesn't matter, anyway. They're cutting me out."

"What do you mean?"

"You can recognize it, just like anyone else," said Tabby. "When people have cooled on you. Maybe they just didn't like how I reacted to the cow. But they come to me less and less often for help. More and more to my team, who now are about as well versed on the tech as I am. I'm obsolete."

Jon shook his head. "I still don't get why my news made you more afraid."

"Think about it, Jon," said Tabby. "Do you think it's an accident Shaw mentioned soldiers? The end of trauma? Please. I'm sure he'd like you to believe that he'd give your tech to everyone, free, for ally and enemy alike, but I don't believe it for a second."

"But that's the whole pitch of this place," said Jon. "It's saving the world."

"The whole place is a lie," said Tabby. "Shaw never intended to save anything. We don't even know what's actually happening on the surface. Everything could be back to normal for all we know. He's kept us afraid and in the dark, and we've been creating new technologies for him, for free."

"And now he can take them, and sell them to the highest bidder," said Jon.

"I don't think that's his plan," said Tabby. "Although it's no better."

"What's his plan, then?" asked Jon.

"What did he tell you about the soldiers?" asked Tabby.

"He said to imagine a soldier who's been shot, or been blown up. Imagine their wound healing on the battlefield, completely. Maybe with the help of a single medic, if there are complications. He said that it would end all conflict."

Tabby stared at him. "Here. Imagine this, instead. Imagine one army, all members functionally invincible. Able to heal bullet wounds, and explosions, and god knows anything else on the battlefield, within a couple minutes. Imagine that same army with advanced weaponry, that is nearly silent, has impossible range, and incredible firepower. And now, imagine that same army equipped with all the technology down here that you and I have no idea about. Armors, explosives, who knows what. All supported by unparalleled systems funded by the richest man on Earth."

"Fuck," said Jon.

"Exactly," said Tabby. "He is preparing for the end of the world, Jon. God knows how long he's had this plan, but it's been a long time. He's seen the writing on the wall, and he bided his time, and gathered resources. Managed his persona and brand. Used his natural charisma to sway anyone he couldn't win over with money."

"It was all the lie," said Jon. "I can't help him, then. I can't help give him more power."

"I've heard word of a resistance," said Tabby. "Only whispers, though."

"Down here? Like Armitage?"

"I don't really know if Armitage even did anything," said Tabby. "He could have been a false flag. Just like the nuclear attack. Something to deflect attention from his true motives."

"I don't know what to do," said Jon. "I don't want to help him."

"At this point," said Tabby. "Does your team even need you?"

"I don't know," said Jon. "I still have some know-how that Stone and others don't."

"What about the rest of your team?" asked Tabby. "Can you protect them?"

"I can try," said Jon.

"Then that's what you do," said Tabby. "Try and stick around as long as you can. And maybe we can sabotage something, somewhere. I think that's our best choice. We can't do anything if we're dead. Not to mention Tommy. I doubt Shaw would still care about him if you were gone."

Jon's heart hurt at the thought. He nodded. "I'll do my best. But I can't sandbag. Shaw is watching me like a hawk."

"Well, he still wants his arm back," said Tabby. "That hasn't changed. That arm is as part of his image as anything is, and if the first picture back is him with a new arm? That's all the news will see."

"I thought we were saving the world," said Jon, his head in his hands.

"We've never been saving the world," said Tabby. "We're working on taking it over."

21

Jon wasn't affected by the rats. The mutations bothered him; the failure bothered him, but he didn't carry a rat's death home with him. There were too many of them. It would break him if he allowed it.

The chimps were a different story. Failing with them went home with him. He didn't know when the line was crossed, but seeing the chimpanzees mutate, removing a limb and then watching it grow back into some terrible monstrous thing—it hurt. And the hurt stayed with him, no matter how many animals they destroyed.

But he could rationalize it, even then. It was for the greater good. It was for boys like Tommy, who would never walk again otherwise. Many others, who through no fault of their own, would be disabled for the rest of their lives.

Shaw's monologue about the cost of a chimpanzee life rang true in that. A human life was more precious than a thousand chimps.

But this? This he couldn't stomach. Just the thought of it made his guts ache, and he felt a migraine growing in his head. His body was telling him to do whatever was necessary to stop this from happening, to take the bullet for the cause.

But Jon knew that wouldn't matter. If he stepped down, Stone would step into his place. Hell, he already was. Stone was enthusiastic in all the ways that Jon was not. He was happy to draw up plans about how to torture chimps, to inflict trauma on them, and see how they regrew. Jon looked into Stone's eyes, and he didn't know what was there. What drove him? Was it sheer fear of Shaw? Was it blind ambition? Was it pleasure from inflicting pain? Jon didn't know, but in the end it didn't matter. If Jon was removed, the only change would be less oversight, and less protection for Mel. Tabby was right. He'd have to hold on.

Sherman gave them everything they needed. They had moved into a new lab, twice as large, with a huge experiment area, modular, protected by blast shields. Sherman also sourced them various firing range protections. He also gave them armed guards. Two of them inside, two of them outside. No matter how long they stood there, Jon couldn't get used to them. They were quiet, and did their job, but Jon kept envisioning them turning their guns on him. One order from Shaw, and it was him in the firing range.

"Jon," said Stone, raising his voice slightly. It jolted Jon from his thoughts.

"Sorry," said Jon.

"We need to push the chimps further," said Stone. "It's the only way we can progress with live testing on the scale Shaw wants. We need to push everything harder."

"We still don't know what the long-term effects are. We just fixed the last chimp, but we don't know if the changes to it are stable. If it can even withstand further injury, or further trauma? It won't always have a nutrient bath. What if it gets injured again? It could trigger further mutation—"

"Shaw doesn't care, Jon, you know that. We need to push it harder."

"I don't know how," said Jon. "They'll burn up. And live testing means no nutrient bath. We have to both accelerate the healing process and do it without dunking them in concentrated nutrients. That's the only reason it's worked so far. If they're conscious, they will resist everything. They won't stay in a nutrient bath, and they certainly won't just let us hurt them, in whatever manner we choose."

"How many calories in the nutrient bath?" asked Stone. "How many do they use?"

"Roughly fifty thousand," said Jon. "Give or take, depending on the overall size of the animal."

"That's a lot of calories," said Stone. "If they're conscious, we can feed them."

"Yes, but a chimp's stomach can't absorb that many calories," said Jon. "And they won't eat willingly. And—"

"Okay, okay," said Stone. "But it is the only way we're going to be able to give them anything. We can restrain them, against a wall. Build an enclosure around them. Administer the serum, deliver trauma, and then fill it with the nutrient solution. They'll absorb it through their skin, just like before. We'll be safe, and the animal won't be able to thrash around."

"It'll still thrash around—"

"Well, some can't be helped—"

"Some can't be helped? It could damage the animal further and make our results even harder to replicate—"

"What do you think we're doing, Jon?" asked Stone, raising his voice. Stone stared at him with his cold eyes, and Jon didn't answer. Shaw had given his directive, and they were to follow it. There was no other way.

"I know," said Jon. "That sounds as good as anything. But we still have to adjust for the amount of damage we're inflicting."

"I'm telling you, we open it up," said Stone. "Increase the bandwidth. Rate of regeneration, rate of absorption, broaden the skin's tolerance threshold—"

"Didn't you say that would lead to side effects?" asked Jon.

"It can," said Stone.

"Like what?"

"Elasticity in the skin," said Stone. "All of this comes from hagfish, and so their skin would emulate that. It's not out of place in a sea creature, but on a mammal? The skin becomes more and more permeable, to allow for greater absorption rates. It will recognize a wider range of things as food, more or less."

"When do we recognize that what we're turning this animal into is no longer a chimp?" asked Jon. The question hung in the air, a silence between the two of them.

"What are our other options?" asked Stone. "If we want to increase the speed of this, these are our choices. Efficiency will only shave off a few minutes. This is what Shaw wants. We have to give it to him."

Jon balanced the thoughts in his head. Stone was right. They had exhausted their playbook, and the only way to make the process faster was to push the chimp's systems to their limit.

No, that's not right. We have to turn it into something else.

"What do you suggest?" asked Jon.

"We dial everything up," said Stone. "All the way. See what we get."

Jon sighed, but nodded. "Okay. And for the trauma?"

"Shaw talked about soldiers, on the front lines. I say we start with a bullet."

"A bullet?"

"One gunshot," said Stone. "To the gut. A survivable wound site." The thought immediately turned Jon's stomach to acid, and he felt the bile rise in his throat. He swallowed it back down.

They got the team together and started building models, assessing the new accelerated serum. They also built the testing rig, where they could restrain the animal, be safe from their own gunfire, and make it watertight, able to hold the nutrient bath.

Mel pulled him aside.

"Are we really doing this?" she asked. Her eyes were wide and full of emotion.

"Yes," said Jon.

"We can't," said Mel. "These aren't rats, Jon. They won't be sedated, and we're just shooting them? I didn't join this team to be a part of a firing squad."

Jon looked in her eyes, and then looked down, unable to meet her gaze for long. "Neither did I," said Jon, finally. He looked around. The rest of the team worked. The two guards stood there, passively. He felt the electric eyes of the cameras on him. How powerful were their microphones?

He leaned into Mel, whispering in her ear.

"Have you noticed how emptier this place is? Shaw is removing people, one by one. And we *will* be next if we don't play ball. I don't know what else to do. They'll take Tommy."

He leaned back and looked again into Mel's eyes. A tear flowed from one eye and she quickly wiped it away. She held eye contact and then nodded.

"You don't have to watch," said Jon. "Make an excuse. Work on the models. I know it's not that much better, but it's something."

Mel nodded again and went back to her workstation. Jon sighed and looked through the batch of the latest models. The greatest hits of the model still stayed stable, despite how hard they had pushed the accelerator. It boggled Jon's mind. How flexible was the DNA of this animal? How far could they push it without complete cell collapse? The advanced CRISPR software helped, filling in the gaps whenever necessary. And even if there wasn't cell collapse, would the thing coming out on the other side even still be a chimp?

Jon tried to hold off the first experiment, but with the modeling results coming in, he couldn't push it off for very long. Shaw's eyes were on him, and he felt the pressure building. They had bought some time with their success, but Shaw's patience would only last so long.

Still, this was only the initial test. They would have time to do more. They would need it. Jon expected little from the first experiment, except suffering for the chimp. He still held that he didn't think the chimp's body could handle how far they were pushing it. If it succeeded at all, he thought the chimp's heart very well might explode, or it could suffer an aneurysm. Every creature had a limit, and they were getting dangerously close to reaching it.

But he let Stone have it. Maybe a failure with this chimp would give them some leeway to dial it back.

Jon's stomach roiled as they brought the first chimp out for the test. Mel stayed at her workstation, working on the next model. He could see the distress on her face. Jon himself would watch, no different from before. This was his project, and he would bear the burden of the memory.

They restrained the animal, strapping its arms and legs to the wall with tight leather restraints, doubled over. And then another over its torso, and then its hips. It wouldn't be able to move much, which would increase the chance of survival. It murmured complaints as they strapped it down, but it still largely remained docile. These chimps were bred for testing, and had their wilder traits removed.

A biologist went in and slid the serum home, and instantly it rewrote the chimp's genetic code. It bellowed. What did it feel like, your DNA being snipped and rewritten, overwritten? Reassembled? DNA had no nerves, so it wouldn't hurt, but the body's changes had to be felt. Jon could see it, the skin softening, a translucent sheen covering the animal.

"Fill it with the nutrient bath," said Stone, and they did, closing the enclosure, sealing it, and then pumping in gallon after gallon of the milky white substance. The enclosure filled, covering the chimp up to its waist. It was confused now, looking around, unsure of what to do, or what was happening to it.

Jon could barely breathe, forcing the air in and out.

Your breath is a swinging door. Your breath is a swinging door.

He tried to stay calm, but his heart raced away. The chimp had suffered nothing yet.

There was debate about what kind of gun to use, and who would fire it. None of the scientists were marksmen. Jon and Stone eventually settled on one of the guards, using their assault rifles. They were trained in the weapon, and it would represent something found on a battlefield. So one of their guards waited nearby, for his signal to line up a shot.

The area behind the chimp was absorbent, able to capture any stray bullets, but Jon didn't expect the guard to miss. The chimp stood only ten feet away and wasn't moving. It was an easy shot.

Not easy. Simple.

The nutrient liquid finally stopped pumping in, and Stone waved the guard over. Stone relayed instructions to him again, and the man coolly nodded. Everyone backed away, behind the shields, and the guard adopted a firing stance, pulled his rifle to his shoulder, and flicked off the safety.

Jon held his breath and plugged his ears with his fingers.

BANG.

He fired one shot, and it hit the chimp in the torso with a dull thud between the leather restraints of its upper torso and hips. It screamed in pain, the noise of the gunshot still echoing in the space. The guard flicked the safety of his rifle on again, and he stepped back, waiting for further instructions from Stone. The chimp screamed, blood leaking out from the hole in its stomach. Jon swallowed vomit.

And then the nutrient bath lowered. Fast.

"Pump more in!" yelled Stone, and they pumped in more of the solution, gallons at a time. The regeneration necessary for a gunshot wound was different than a limb, theoretically requiring fewer calories, but they were taking no chances, giving the chimp as much fuel as it could need.

The chimp screamed, even as it absorbed more and more of the liquid. Something was happening, but the wound was mostly internal, impossible to gauge its progress. Was it working? Was it healing?

And then the bullet was pushed back out of the wound, pieces of lead floating in the bath.

"Oh my God," said Stone, and then the wound closed up, the chimp still struggling against the leather bands.

"It worked," said Jon.

But the chimp continued to scream.

"It's healed," said Stone. "Why is still screaming?"

The chimp thrashed against its restraints even harder, and the nutrient bath continued to lower. Something was wrong, something was wrong.

Jon watched the body of the ape. It bulged, the same distentions, the same mutations as before. From inside, its torso grew, and then its chest, and he could trace it along the veins of the animal, filtering out from the wound site, out into its arms and legs.

The animal screamed even louder, and louder, and Jon couldn't bear it, and it thrashed against its restraints.

"Stop the pumps! Stop the pumps!" yelled Stone. The nutrient bath lowered then, as there was nothing replenishing it, as the chimp continued to exhaust it. Then it was empty. But the chimp still thrashed.

"What do we do?" asked Stone, looking at Jon. Jon

only shook his head, he didn't know, he didn't know. Stone grabbed the guard. "Shoot it! Finish it!"

The guard again took a firing stance, pulling the rifle quickly to his shoulder, and flicked off the safety. He fired three shots in quick succession.

BANG BANG BANG

The shots hit the animal in the chest. The rifle was powerful, and they should have taken the creature down, but it only screamed louder, and then the pieces of lead fell out of the chimp, tinking on the ground.

"It's healing," said Jon.

"Fire again!" yelled Stone.

The guard raised his rifle one more time.

Then the chimp broke its restraints, fast, faster than Jon could track, and it charged the guard, screaming in pain.

22

The guard fired his rifle more as the chimp charged.

BANG

BANG

BANG

BANG

BANG

Quick shots all landed, peppering the chimp with powerful rounds. But it didn't stop, its body still healing, growing, the creature already bigger. It climbed over the shield in a quick movement, fast, and landed on the guard. The guard tried to put the rifle between them but it was gone in an instant, thrown away by the chimp who clawed at him, pulling away the thick layers of kevlar that protected him.

Within moments the man was unprotected, and the

chimp dug its teeth into the guard's neck, and a gout of blood shot out. The chimp didn't stop, pulling away at his flesh, ripping him apart.

Jon knew he should run, run and do something, but he couldn't. He could only stare, because the chimp was doing more than just attacking the guard.

He was *absorbing* him.

As the chimp's skin contacted the guard, the two surfaces melded together, the creature's skin digesting the guard, pulling more and more away with every swipe. The chimp continued to grow, and the lead from the third volley of bullets fell out of him, falling onto the ground.

The guard was dead now, but the chimp kept feeding, both with its mouth and with its skin, rapidly pulling away the flesh of the body, as the guard and the chimp became one.

Don't call it that. It's not a chimp anymore.

And Jon was right. It was twice its original size, its limbs extending, growing, thicker, bone and muscle pushing through the skin. Jon could still see the chimp somewhere inside it, but it was quickly becoming eclipsed by the horrible thing.

Jon looked at the guard again, and within a minute, half his body was gone, absorbed by the creature.

Jon glanced around, and the lab was in chaos, everyone either looking for a weapon or running for the door. More guards came rushing in, the one remaining from inside, and the two others. They saw the thing absorbing their co-worker, and they all opened fire, firing three-round bursts into the creature. Jon dove for cover.

They filled the room with gunfire, but the thing wouldn't

go down, as round after round hit it with wet meaty thuds. It charged the three, pouncing on one and grabbing its weapon, throwing it away. It knew the source of its pain. It thrust a clawed arm into the neck of the disarmed guard, and then dragged the body with him as he attacked a second, swiping away the gun with its other distended arm and then swinging hard into the man's body. The creature had doubled mass, and with it, so had its strength, and the man flew into the wall, grunting.

The third guard continued to fire, burst after burst, but the creature didn't stop healing, now absorbing tissue from the first guard, the meat at the end of its arm a font of nutrients, pumped directly into the engine that had taken it over.

The creature leapt onto him, mounting him, and its free arm ripped him apart, pulling off his armor and flesh alike, sinking the arm deep into his body. It stood there, absorbing the meat, healing the many gunshot wounds, growing ever larger. It now stood seven feet tall. It still shared the gait of the chimp it once was, but there was nothing else recognizable anymore. Its body was a mass of muscle, bone, and flesh, pulsating, searching for more to feed on. The process had taken it over.

The second guard had gotten to his feet, and tried to run, but the creature threw away the body of the first, and plunged its arm into its new victim, melding with him now. Within moments, he was dead.

Jon looked, seeing Stone across the room, hiding, just as Jon had. The thing fed for a few moments more, but soon the bodies of the guards were depleted, and it thrust them down, screaming an incredible guttural noise, a noise that knew no home. The creature smashed through the doors to the experiment area, charging out into the open hallways of the dark lab. Jon's mind raced. They had to stop it or it would kill them all. It only wanted to feed.

"We have to kill it," said Jon, scrambling to his feet, helping Stone up.

"How?" asked Stone.

"We need a killshot," said Jon.

"That won't work on that thing," said Stone.

"Not a normal killshot," said Jon. "A CRISPR scrambler. Destroy it at a cellular level."

Jon raced after it, hearing calamity ahead. His mind went to his team, to Mel. He heard more gunshots. More guards had arrived. At least they could distract it, but in the end, they were only more food.

Their lab was a mess, with upturned tables. Several members of the team lay nearby. Jon looked for Mel. He spotted her hiding under a lab table near her workstation. He ran to her.

"What is that?" asked Mel. "Is that the chimp?"

"Not anymore," said Jon. Stone followed behind him. "We need a serum. A scrambler. It needs to cut apart the creature's DNA. It's the only thing that can take it down."

Mel nodded and went to her workstation. "It will take a few minutes." More gunshots rang out and then stopped. The alarm rang then, and the room was bathed in red.

EMERGENCY LOCKDOWN IN EFFECT
EMERGENCY LOCKDOWN IN EFFECT
EMERGENCY LOCKDOWN IN EFFECT

The familiar voice rang out.

"I don't think some locked doors are going to stop that thing," said Stone.

Jon left Stone with Mel and went to the outer door of their lab. The creature had left chaos in its wake. Half digested bodies were strewn everywhere, blood and gore piled around them. The thing had gone from body to body, absorbing what it could, before moving onto the next.

Louder gunshots rang out now. Shotguns. Jon followed the trail of blood. He should have turned around, but he needed to see. Just like he needed to watch the experiment. He had to bear the burden of his creation.

He crept through the hallways of the labs, a path of destruction laid out in front of him. Bodies were strewn about, the glass walls of the various labs broken, shattered. A few researchers ran past him as he followed the creature.

And then he saw it. Saw what it had become.

It was massive now, ten feet tall, and six or seven feet across. But its size had finally hurt it, as it moved slower, the incredible mutative growth making it more and more immobile.

It was nearly invincible though, proven by the shotgun blasts it absorbed. An entire squad of guards had surrounded it, all protected in riot gear and pump action shotguns. They unloaded blast after blast directly into it, and blood and bone flew off the creature in sprays behind it, covering the area with gore.

But it didn't slow down, lumbering after each guard, and now not attacking, but enveloping them as a whole.

It swallowed one, the guard suffocating in the creature's mass. He screamed, screamed for help, until flesh filled his lungs. The other guards unloaded on it, but it did nothing. It came after the next, and the others ran. Ran toward him.

Oh shit.

The creature turned and moved after them, and it saw Jon now, its face a mass of flesh and cartilage, two eyes still peering out, the only original thing remaining. It saw Jon, and it lumbered toward him. Flesh and bone and muscle sprung from it as it ran, regenerating what was lost and more, and he sprinted back to his lab. He hoped they had the shot; they needed it now.

Jon turned and ran, but he heard it behind him, smashing its way through glass partitions and doors, upending tables and equipment. Some of it got absorbed in its mass of flesh, bits of metal and glass poking out. He looked back to see it, closer now, still moving, faster than him, even with its size.

Jon sprinted as hard as he could, wishing he had spent more time on the treadmill. He saw his lab, and he hoped they had the shot ready.

It gained on him, and he could hear the shuffling of the flesh as it chased him, bone and muscle scraping against the ground. They had made this thing; they had to kill it, before it destroyed everything down here.

He ran for the outer doors of his lab, and Stone and Mel waited there. Stone held the tranquilizer rifle to his shoulder.

"Shoot it!" yelled Jon, sprinting past them. Stone pulled the trigger, and Jon turned to see the dart shoot out and land in the middle of the mass of the great creature. It screamed, its body an amplifier, and Jon heard nothing but it. It still charged, only thirty feet away. It would be on them in an instant, and it would absorb them, and they would become a part of its great mass. It was an ending they deserved. They had created this thing and becoming a part of it was justice.

It lumbered, but then the scrambler took a hold of it from within, and it slowed, the great scrabbling legs stumbled, pieces of flesh sloughing off from it as its cellular walls collapsed. The distended bone and muscle softened, and then melted, cell by cell, and the creature then fell, as its legs disintegrated beneath it. It slid toward them, still screaming in pain.

The creature's flesh liquefied in front of them, and its great size diminished, slowly turning into a puddle on the floor, pieces of body armor and lab equipment mixed among it. Jon thought he could spot pieces of the original chimp in there somewhere, but he wasn't sure. It had absorbed over a dozen people along the way, and their flesh was there too, converted into regenerative cells. The smell hit him then, and Jon retched, unable to stop himself.

He threw up to the side, the impossible stink of bile and blood overpowering his senses. It was a new smell, a smell of wrongness. He wiped his mouth.

The creature was mostly gone now, turned into a puddle of mixed regenerative flesh. It squelched and bubbled, as it was broken down into its most basic elements.

"Jesus fucking Christ," said Stone. He fell to his knees. Mel and Jon only stared at what remained of the thing.

A team of guards approached cautiously, two dozen of them, armed with shotguns and riot shields, the only equipment they had to deal with resistance.

"It's dead," said Jon, to the guard leading them. "It's dead."

23

Shaw scrubbed through footage of the creature. Back and forth, back and forth. The footage cut to different security cameras, as the creature was born, attacked guards, grew, rampaged, and finally died.

He watched it, over and over again, while Jon sat and waited. Jon didn't watch, not now. He had already seen it, and it replayed in his mind endlessly, the creature absorbing the guards.

It had taken hours to clean the lab. Dozens were dead, including half his team, killed in the immediate rampage. Multiple clean-up crews appeared within minutes, bagging up bodies. Jon didn't know where they had come from, or where they took the bodies. He didn't ask, not expecting an answer either way. Doctors saw to them, to him, Stone, Mel, the rest of the survivors. The three of them were fine, aside from some bumps and bruises. Most of the survivors hadn't been touched at all. One had survived with broken ribs after being thrown to the side, but all who had been touched by the creature had died, eviscerated or absorbed.

They collected the massive pile of flesh, people in white hazmat suits collecting it in vials, in bags, in bottles. But none was disposed of. Jon didn't know what kind of scientific value it had, if any at all. The CRISPR scrambler had most likely destroyed any evidence of what happened inside the creature after their test, and they still had the serum on file. They could make another, make a thousand of them.

Jon didn't know what to expect from Shaw. He wanted results, but this thing had killed dozens of his workers, and damaged part of his facility. It was monstrous, disastrous. He had exiled Armitage for setting off a small firebomb that ultimately hurt no one and damaged nothing.

So Jon had stepped into Shaw's office the next day expecting the worst. He had hugged Tommy extra hard that morning before leaving, just in case. He wanted something else he could do, some fallback plan, but there was nothing. His ultimate arbiter stood in front of him, examining camera footage, repeatedly.

Shaw finally looked to him.

"What happened, Jon?" asked Shaw. "In your own words."

"After a certain point, I don't really know," said Jon.

"Start at the beginning," said Shaw.

"Well, Dr. Stone and I talked about your expectations, and we tried to meet them. You wanted battlefield testing, so that's what we settled on. A gunshot wound, fired by an assault rifle. And we shaped almost everything else around that. How we conducted the experiment, how we restrained the subject."

Jon looked to Shaw, trying to gauge his reaction, but he still scrubbed through the footage, back and forth, back and forth.

"The other was the speed of regeneration," said Jon. "We'd seen mutation before, both in the rats and in the chimps, and it always was because of mis-matches in the rate of re-construction and the amount of cells required for that re-generation. The fire can only burn so hot without enough fuel, and without it, it sputters, and causes deformity, which then chain react, and spin off from the core DNA pattern. Until this point, the subject has always been unconscious, unable to do anything but lie there, as its body mutated. We've always stopped the experiments at that point. Dissections have never given us anything conclusive."

"What caused it to—to absorb the flesh of others?" asked Shaw.

"Dr. Stone's research was always centered on skin permeability," said Jon. "An ability the hagfish has, where it can digest through its epidermis. A unique ability, which could have a lot of applications in medicine. We used it to up the caloric absorption rate of the subjects up to this point. Our goal was to increase the rate of regeneration by significant margins, so we made meaningful changes to the serum. We accelerated the reconstruction rate, and to fuel it, we upped the digestion rate. And more than that, we lowered the threshold for caloric response by the skin."

"So, if I understand you, you told the skin to recognize more things as food," said Shaw. "And coupled with the permeability of the epidermis, and it's accelerated regeneration rate, it could absorb human flesh, and convert that into stem cells?" asked Shaw. His eyes had turned to Jon, his plastic face betraying nothing. The security footage still played on a screen in front of him. On it, the creature absorbed a guard, armor and all, and Jon looked away.

"Yes," said Jon. "More or less. But there's a lot of things in there that I don't understand how or why they happened. The way it grew, the speed at which it absorbed flesh—I really wouldn't know unless I could look at the creature afterward. But that's impossible. Or, by recreating the test, which I don't think anyone wants."

Shaw scrubbed through the footage again, back to where the guards were pelting the creature with shotgun blasts, which had no noticeable effect on its health.

Beautiful," said Shaw, finally. "The chimpanzee soaked up 37 point blank shotgun blasts. 37. And another 95 rounds from assault rifles. Just an astounding amount of damage. Enough to kill dozens of men. And it shrugged it all off. Even better, it *absorbed* it. He took the damage, and just kept going."

Jon studied Shaw's face and realized he was happy.

"This is what I was talking about," said Shaw. "A chimpanzee absorbed hundreds of bullet wounds, and was none the worse for wear. It took out a dozen armed guards, and could have stopped many more. A pity you had to take it down before we could see what it was truly capable of, but oh well. It was only the first test."

"It killed dozens of innocent people," said Jon.

Shaw ignored him. "Imagine, Jon. Imagine, one more time. Imagine, that thing, on a battlefield. That creation, let loose upon a city of enemy combatants. It would wreak havoc. Even if you could stop it, it would take dozens of men, and thousands of rounds of ammunition. Now imagine, dozens. Or hundreds of them. You could take down a city full of soldiers within days."

Jon stared at him. Shaw's eyes had gone wide, glistening. Shaw licked his lips.

"But it's incredibly unstable," said Jon. "There's no coming back from that kind of transformation. There's no quality of life."

Shaw looked at him, askance. "You can iron that out, though, can't you, Jon? You've done so much, in so little time. You crawled at first, but now you run, covering vast ground within days. I don't know why I ever doubted you. I was going to ask you, regardless of the result, but now I feel more confident than ever. It's time to move forward, again."

"What?" asked Jon. "How? We've had one test, and it was disastrous."

"This is not disaster, Jon," said Shaw. "This is raw, limitless potential. I want to push forward. I want to move onto human testing."

"That's impossible," said Jon.

"Why?" asked Shaw. "This is not the surface, Jon. I make the rules down here. Why wait years for human efficacy tests, when a medication could save lives today?"

"There's good reason for that," said Jon. "It can cost human lives."

"Big ideas require small sacrifices," said Shaw.

"That's easy to say when it's not your life," said Jon. He felt the anger rising in his gut, the same as when he fought with Stone. An anger that had built for months now. Shaw had pushed them, and pushed them, and now it had cost human lives, and now he wanted more.

Shaw stared at him, confused. He wasn't used to having anger directed at him.

"Watch yourself, Jon," said Shaw. "Don't forget who I am."

"I haven't forgotten," said Jon. "I know who you are. We all do, very intimately. You're Eaton Shaw. The richest man in the world. Who has built his own fiefdom, deep underground, so that he can harvest research and technology from the world's best and brightest, and utilize it in any way he sees fit. You're Eaton Shaw, the man who lured hundreds of people down into an unknown fortress with promises of heroism. You're Eaton Shaw, who lied to them all, to get the fruits of their labor, and then erased them when they were of no more use, or when they dared to disobey you."

Shaw narrowed his eyes. "You have no—"

"Human testing is not only impossible, it's irresponsible. I can't do this anymore. I won't do it anymore. Go find someone else. Go ask Stone. Maybe he'll be willing to forget his ethics so you'll let him live another day, but I'm not. I'm not doing this anymore."

Shaw stared at him, and then looked down and sighed.

"I really thought you understood, Jon," said Shaw. "It's too bad."

Jon felt movement behind him, and two armed guards were there, had been there. They waited.

"I haven't killed anyone, Jon," said Shaw. "Most of the researchers who've finished their work are under house arrest. It was the best solution I could come up with. I can't have them going back to the surface and revealing what they know. Not yet."

"Most," said Jon.

"My most trusted are working in the world, getting things ready for implementation. Large-scale manufacturing is untenable down here. Not so on the surface. I'm not an idiot. I'm not going to destroy valuable resources. Not unless absolutely necessary."

"Why did you lie about the nuclear attack?" asked Jon. He felt the presence of the assault rifles, a threat.

"Just to provide some urgency to the teams still working," said Shaw. "A few were lagging behind. Like yourself. I thought it would help. And it did. We've had multiple breakthroughs since I disseminated the news."

"The ends justify the means," said Jon.

"Well, yes, obviously," said Shaw. "A little extra motivation works wonders. And it's why you're going to continue to help me with your research, and it is also why we are going to move onto human testing."

"You can't *make* me," said Jon.

"Oh, Jon," said Shaw. "Of course I can. Why do you think Tommy is down here?"

Jon's heart went cold.

"Do you think I invited anyone's family out of the kindness of my heart? They are a resource, just like you are, and I will use that resource if necessary."

"You bastard—" Jon coiled, ready to charge at Shaw.

"Nuh uh uh," said Shaw, waggling his metallic finger at Jon. "Don't make me hurt you."

"You better hope—"

"Oh, please," said Shaw. "Stop with your threats. I am out of your purview. If it wasn't clear before, it should be now. I have a deal for you, Jon."

Jon stared. He wanted to kill Shaw, to deliver even a fraction of the punishment the chimp had received. But he felt the rifles at his back.

"Hear me out," said Shaw. "Tommy is a perfect test subject. He's young, and strong. He's very healthy, aside from his missing legs. And you are very motivated to see him survive. So I want you to give him his legs back. Very simple. He is a test case. You did it to a chimp, I'm certain you can make it work on Tommy."

"What if I refuse?" asked Jon.

"Then we'll take him, and do it anyway, without you," said Shaw. "Those are your options. Do you trust Dr. Stone to oversee the operation? Because if you do not take part, he almost certainly will be in charge of your son's life. I think we both know that you're a more capable scientist than him. Don't you agree?"

Jon's heart thumped hard inside his chest. Tears welled in the corners of his eyes.

"Well, Jon, what's your answer?" asked Shaw. "We don't have time for deliberation."

"You know my answer," said Jon, finally.

"Good," said Shaw. "I'll let you break the news to Tommy. You have a week."

Jon stood up, walking out of Shaw's office. Shaw spoke to him as he walked away.

"I told you, Jon. Remember, when you first arrived?" asked Shaw. "I told you Tommy will walk out of this lab, on his own two feet. And with your help, he will."

24

Jon waited until the last possible moment to tell Tommy. He gave him as much peace of mind as he could, but despite that, the week flew by.

Jon stole every moment and spent it with Tommy. He made Tommy's favorite food for dinner every night, and he played video games with him, even though Jon was terrible. Still, he was strapped for time, and he slept little for that week. When Tommy when to bed, Jon was up again, and back at the lab, crunching all the numbers.

He wasn't alone. The rest of his team was working, and Shaw didn't try to sandbag him. He gave him more assistants, replacing those killed by the chimp, and assigning even more to his team. Jon needed all the help he could get, giving Mel free rein to delegate roles. She carried a lot of responsibility, because they only had one shot at this, and her models were going to bear the brunt of the work.

"I want to thank you," said Jon. "For everything."

It was late at night, or early in the morning. Jon had lost track of his schedule. He was taking ADHD medicine to focus, stealing a few hours of sleep before getting back to work. He and Mel were the only ones in the lab. It was the night before they would operate on Tommy.

"Jon, you don't—"

"Yes, I do," said Jon. "I wouldn't want anyone else helping me. If we ever get out of here—I owe you a beer."

"I actually prefer ciders," said Mel.

"You would," said Jon.

"Nothing wrong with a good cider," said Mel. "I'd kill for one right around now."

"I'm sure Shaw could get you one," said Jon.

"I've only been using the bare essentials," said Mel. "I want to use his things as little as possible. Does—does Tommy know yet?"

"No," said Jon. "I don't know how to tell him. Part of me wants to wait until the last feasible moment. How would you feel? Taken against your will, to be a guinea pig? I could tell him now, but then he gets days of dread before it happens. And there's no negotiation. If he struggles or resists, they'll take him anyway. They don't care. I can't stop them. They have all the power."

"I wish I could do something," said Mel. She looked up to a camera. "You think he's listening?"

"Oh, probably," said Jon. "I don't care anymore."

"Have you talked to Tabby?" asked Mel.

"Not in days," said Jon. "She's under house arrest. Her

project is done. I don't have the keys. I tried to go to her floor, but Nadia didn't grant me permission."

"The eye in the sky doesn't lie," said Mel, quietly.

"What's that?"

"Oh, I don't know," said Mel. "A fragment from a song I used to know."

"How are the models looking?"

"They're as about as fine-tuned as I can make them," said Mel. "The jump from chimp to human isn't as extreme as rat to chimp, but we're not the same, still. At least Shaw isn't being so strict about his requirements on this."

"This is a test case for him. He wants it to succeed, and he doesn't want to turn into a monster, like the chimp did. I'm sure he's fine with pumping that into soldiers, but he doesn't want to mutate. He wants his arm back."

"It's made it easier," said Mel. "But there's still so many variables. Humans are not chimps."

"No," said Jon. He put his head down on the table and closed his eyes. "I need to sleep. I need to be fresh for tomorrow. Is there anything left to do tonight to increase our chances of success?"

"I don't think so," said Mel. "If anyone can think of it, they're smarter than me. I have something else, though."

"What's that?"

"I built another formula. A reset formula. A zero formula. If something goes wrong with Tommy tomorrow, like what happened with the chimp—"

"I don't want to even think about it," said Jon.

"Well, if it happens, it should reset his biology back to default."

"Will it work, if it comes to it?"

"It should," said Mel. "But we won't know until we use it, for sure. There's no way to test it."

"I hope it doesn't come to it."

"I hope it doesn't either."

"I'll see you tomorrow," said Jon.

"We can do this," said Mel. "And we will."

Jon smiled and hugged her and then went back to his home. As he exited the elevator, Nadia's voice surprised him.

"Sleep well, Doctor. Good luck tomorrow," she said, and the door closed. *Strange.*

His home was dark and quiet. Tommy slept in his room. He could wake him now and tell him, but what purpose would that serve? If he must hurt his son, he would make it as painless as he could.

Jon peeked into his room and watched him sleep for a moment, his chest gently rising and falling. He looked to his wheelchair, empty, next to Tommy's bed. Tomorrow would be the last time he used it, whatever the result.

Jon laid down, and then his alarm was ringing. His body desperately wanted more sleep, but he forced his feet to the floor, and took more pills to wake him up, and to keep him awake. It was six AM, and he would need to wake Tommy.

His stomach ached, and he tried to force himself to go in and wake him up, but he couldn't, his hand frozen before it opened Tommy's door. Then the door notification rang, and he realized the guards were already there. He went to the door. Four men, stern faced, waited with assault rifles.

"Please, give me ten minutes," said Jon. "I want to try and have him go peacefully, okay? It will make your job easier." The one in charge eyed him and then nodded.

Jon strode back to Tommy's room, forcing himself to

go inside. Tommy was sitting up in bed, wiping away sleep from his eyes. The door had woken him up.

"Who is it? What time is it?" he asked. Jon closed his door behind him and sat down at the edge of his bed.

"You know I love you, right?" asked Jon.

"Yeah, I know," said Tommy. "What's going on?"

Jon sighed, trying to breathe deeply, trying to exhale all the anxiety in his heart. It didn't work, and he cried. He tried to stop himself, but it only made it worse.

"Are you okay?" asked Tommy.

Jon wiped away his tears.

"There are a lot of things that I haven't told you, about this place, Tommy," said Jon. "And we don't have time for it right now. So I need for you to listen. Because there are four armed guards at our front door—"

"What? What are—"

"Please, Tommy," said Jon. "Please listen. There are four armed guards, and they're here for you. They're going to take you down to a lab, and then you're going to get prepped for surgery later today."

"I don't want—"

"It doesn't matter," said Jon. "Believe me. What I wanted flew out the window a long time ago. Shaw wants to test my research on a human subject, and he wants me to help, so he's chosen you."

"What kind of surgery?" asked Tommy.

"Your legs," said Jon. "He wants me to give you your legs back, so he can know it's safe to get his arm back."

Tommy looked at him with fear and anger in his eyes.

"Is it safe?" asked Tommy, finally.

"I don't know," said Jon. "I think so, but you'll be the first test. So I can't guarantee anything. But if I don't agree to help, he'll take you, anyway. And there's no one better than me to oversee this. So please believe me, I don't want this to happen. I want you to be the way you want to be. Please believe me."

"I believe you, Dad," said Tommy. "I'm—I'm scared."

"So am I," said Jon. "It's okay to be afraid."

"I miss Mom," said Tommy. "You think she's safe?"

"Of course," said Jon. "I'd be more afraid for the rest of the world. She's tough. She's an ass-kicker. I should have left you up there with her. You'd be better off."

"I told her," said Tommy.

"Hindsight is 20/20," said Jon. Jon sighed.

"Should I get dressed?" asked Tommy.

"You can wear your pajamas," said Jon. "You'll have to change eventually, but I wouldn't worry about that now. I'm so proud of you."

"Why?" asked Tommy.

"You're so brave," said Jon. "Braver than me."

"You're doing okay, Dad," said Tommy.

"Glowing compliments," said Jon. "Are you ready?"

"Can I use the bathroom first?" asked Tommy.

"Sure," said Jon.

Jon pushed Tommy out of his room a few minutes later. The four guards waited just inside the front door. They looked even larger inside, each of them a mass of black armor, with a sleek assault rifle carried in their arms. Jon had thought this scenario out a thousand times, trying to think of a way to escape with Tommy.

All of them ended in failure. No plot, no scheme would work. There were too many systems that stood between them and the free world.

Tommy didn't cry as he pushed him, and that might have been what pushed Jon over the edge. He felt the heat rise in his chest again, a hard, burning anger, a rage, a frustration, for this terrible situation that he had to face, that Tommy faced bravely. He looked at the four armed guards.

Each of them looked bored. This was just another duty to them, to escort a child in a wheelchair to surgery. Did they question their orders, ever? Even once? Or did they go along because Shaw gave them three hots and a cot?

Jon's anger rose, angry at these men, who did Shaw's bidding without question, who followed orders with confidence, and Jon stopped pushing the wheelchair, staring at the four of them.

"You ready to go?" asked the leader, his rifle hanging loosely in his hands.

Jon couldn't stop himself. He charged him, running at the leader. The look on his face told Jon that he hadn't expected it, but the element of surprise did little to help Jon.

Jon was a scientist. A researcher. He was lucky to finish a mile in under twenty minutes. He rushed the guard, and his movement surprised him, but the guard was young, and fit, and trained. The guard stepped back, grabbed his rifle in two hands, and swung the butt out at Jon as he advanced. It caught him in the temple, and the world turned to black.

25

"Dad, do you have to go back to work tonight?"

Jon looked into the rear-view mirror, seeing Tommy in the back seat. His legs swung freely.

"I'm sorry, kiddo," said Jon. "But I do. I have some work I have to get done."

"You say that every night," said Tommy.

"It's true every night," said Jon. "At least we got to see a movie, just you and me. Did you like it?"

"Yeah, it was great," said Tommy.

"Who was your favorite?" asked Jon.

"Iron Man," said Tommy. "He's funny. It's sad, though."

"It is," said Jon. "But it was for the greater good, right?"

"Yeah, I guess," said Tommy. "He saved the world."

"Right," said Jon. "He saved the world. But in the end, he

saved his daughter."

"Would you save the world for me?" asked Tommy.

"Of course," said Jon. "In a heartbeat."

Jon yawned. He had barely slept the night before, but Maya had been telling him for weeks to spend some time alone with Tommy. So they went and saw the new Avengers movie. Tommy had already seen it, but he was happy to see it again. Jon looked into the rear-view mirror. Tommy had pulled out his Switch, the light illuminating his face.

Jon yawned again. His eyelids were heavy. God, he had a long night ahead of him. The grant paperwork needed to be done tonight. He had put it off long enough. He took a swig of coffee and grimaced at the taste. It was the only thing keeping him going.

He'd had a good time tonight. He missed spending time with the kiddo, but he wouldn't let Maya take all the burden of paying the bills on her shoulders, even if she could handle it. He would do his part, and if that meant some time away from Tommy and her, well, it's a price he would pay. He'd see them this weekend. The grant paperwork would be done by then, and he'd have a little time to relax—

Heavy impact and glass shattering woke him and he was spinning in the air, and then his head hit the airbag, oh god, where's Tommy? Jon's mind tried to make sense of what had happened, but the vehicle was turning in the air, and then he hit the ground with a thud. His knee screamed in pain, wedged between the seat and the dashboard. His head was jammed between airbags, and he couldn't move. The car spun slowly on the ground, and then came to a stop, after what seemed like an eternity.

He was upside down. He hung, his seatbelt holding him

in. The airbag blocked his vision, and he reached for the key, pulled it out of the ignition, and jammed it hard into the bag, popping a hole in it. He could see now, the windshield broken. Everything was upside down, and there was glass everywhere, headlights illuminating.

"He ran the light, I couldn't stop!" yelled a voice, gruff, and deep. Jon blinked, trying to make sense of the world. He saw a shoe. Tommy's shoe, a red Nike, he had wanted the red Nikes for a year, but it didn't make sense. The shoe sat on the ground, and a leg stuck up out of it, but Tommy wasn't—

Oh god, oh god, Tommy

Jon's eyes opened to the sound of Shaw's voice. His head ached with a dull thudding pain.

"Look at the man," said Shaw. "Does he look like a threat to you? He's about to oversee a major operation, and you thought it best to club him in the head. You better hope he wakes up, or your ass—"

Jon sat up, his hand going to the side of his head, feeling the goose egg that had raised on his temple.

"Oh, thank Christ," said Shaw. Shaw looked Jon in the eyes. "You there, Jon?"

"Yeah, I'm here," said Jon. "I need an aspirin."

"You'll get them," said Shaw. "I wouldn't call it smart to charge at the armed guards."

"Sometimes I don't do smart things," said Jon.

"Touche," said Shaw. "Your boy is worried about you."

"He's a good kid," said Jon. "You should let us go."

Shaw smiled. "Are you still capable of overseeing the operation? If not, I'll enlist Dr. Stone to step in—"

"No," said Jon. "I can do it." Jon blinked, trying to clear his head, of both the pain and the memories that had flooded in.

Goddamnit, brain. Not the best time for this shit.

The broken glass, the torn metal. The memory lingered. Jon shoved it away.

"Where's Tommy?" asked Jon.

"He's with the medical team," said Shaw. "They're preparing him. Are you ready?"

"As ready as I'll ever be," said Jon.

"Mr. Johnson will lead the way," said Shaw. "I'll ask that you don't try and attack him again."

"I'll do my best," said Jon. His anger had left him. He could only muster half-assed sarcasm now. He had to focus on the operation. The team was practiced, and prepared, but he would make sure everything went smoothly. He followed Johnson down to the prep room, where Tommy laid on a stretcher.

"Dad!" he yelled, when he saw him. "You're okay." Jon hugged him.

"Yeah, just got a bump on the noggin," said Jon. "I'll be fine. How are you doing?"

"I'm okay," said Tommy, but Jon saw the fear in his eyes. Jon squeezed his hand.

"You're doing great," said Jon. "I have to get ready, okay?"

"Okay," said Tommy. Jon hugged him again.

"I love you," he whispered in Tommy's ear.

"I love you, too," Tommy whispered back.

Jon scrubbed up and got dressed. He wouldn't be doing any of the direct work, but it was still protocol. They were following the same procedure as the successful chimp, only altering the serum. Jon and Stone had settled on it after a lot of discussion. It had worked once before. It should work again. But that's what they had said multiple times before, and failure had resulted.

Shaw looked down on them from the viewing area. Several guards stood there with him, armed with assault rifles, and what Jon guessed were flamethrowers. They had changed their strategy after seeing what the mutated chimp had done. Jon didn't know if fire would be more effective, but Shaw was hedging his bets.

They wheeled Tommy into the operating room. Mel stood by him, holding his hand. Jon caught her eyes and nodded at her.

"You ready, buddy?" asked Jon, standing next to him.

"I guess," said Tommy.

"I'll be the first person you see when you wake up," said Jon.

The anesthesiologist placed a mask over Tommy's mouth and nose.

"Count down from one hundred, Tommy," she said. Tommy counted, and soon he was quiet, unconscious. His vitals beeped on monitors nearby. His heart rate was normal. Jon's wasn't, already thumping hard in his chest.

He tried to control his breathing. His whole body hurt, tired, his head aching, his heart trying to break its way through his breastbone. Jon needed to calm down, or he'd be no use to anyone. Mel grabbed his hand and squeezed, and it helped. He squeezed back.

"Okay," said Jon. "Expose wound sites."

Dr. Stone stood near Tommy's legs, and pulled back the sheet, revealing his two stumps above his knees, one slightly higher than the other. Skin covered both with knots of scar tissue at the end of each. They would reopen the wounds, as if the amputation was fresh, and theoretically, with the help of the serum and the nutrient bath, his body would take over, and regenerate them, like the trauma had happened yesterday.

"Reopen wound sites," said Jon, taking a deep breath. He would make himself watch. He heard glass shattering, metal ripping, the feeling of being weightless before crashing down to earth.

The surgeon cut through the skin and flesh, and blood poured out of Tommy. One assistant sucked it up with a vacuum while another wiped away any remaining with gauze. Jon's stomach bounced around inside him, his only son being opened up again, but he made himself watch. He took deep breaths, his heart pounding.

"Right leg wound site open," said the surgeon who then moved onto the left, doing the same again. Within minutes, the wounds were raw and bloody, blood pouring out of them. Without intervention, Tommy would bleed to death.

"Move him to the nutrient bath," said Jon. They carried him over where his body could lay submerged and his head could stick out. It was a harder proposition, but they managed it, the trail of tubes still leading to Tommy. The nutrients turned pink from Tommy's blood.

"Dr. Stone, inject the serum," said Jon. Stone nodded and shot the mixture into Tommy's upper thigh.

Please.

The nutrient bath level dropped quickly.

"Pump in more nutrient bath," said Jon, trying to keep his voice steady. He felt his hands shaking, and he squeezed them hard. The soft whirr of a pump started, and more of the liquid flowed in, keeping the level constant.

Here's where the rubber meets the road.

Jon's eyes looked at Tommy's legs, the blood flow from the wound sites slowing to an ooze. He watched, and then they healed.

They always heal right at first.

Jon stared, watching the bone slowly knit itself together. He forced breath in and out of his lungs, because if he didn't he would pass out. The two leg bones grew parallel to each other, extending downward, forming the knot that was the knee. Jon waited, waited for a mutation, a deformity. The first sign of any aberration, but there were none yet. Muscle filled in behind the bone, covering it with dark red flesh, woven tightly.

Jon blinked, and behind his eyes he only saw all the terrible potentialities, of Tommy's legs extending, to distend, to bloat and explode into bulbous masses of twisted bone and inflated muscle. But he would open his eyes again to Tommy still healing, the knees formed now, cartilage building, tendons forming in place, tissue covering and intertwining.

Skin had formed, merging with existing skin on his leg, no difference in tone, the same skin, the same skin.

Please.

Jon stared, his eyes tearing. He forced his eyes closed, seeing nightmares, thoughts of a semi-truck tearing his car in half, tearing his son in half, but he pushed them away, forced himself to focus only on Tommy's legs, watching the bone regenerate itself, down to his ankles. Tommy absorbed the nutrients, still, his skin now an active organ, sending the calories into his body, converted into stem cells, converted into bone and muscle and tendon and skin and life.

The ankles were done now, and then Tommy's feet grew.

Jon remembered his feet, remembered playing little piggy with Tommy when he was little. Tommy was ticklish, but only on his toes, and after the accident he had never been tickled again.

The feet formed, even as the muscle slipped down past the knee, forming around the calf, skin following it. Jon waited for calamity. He waited for disaster. It would come late, another twist of the knife, one more punishment for Jon's mistake.

But it didn't come. The bone regrew, finishing the feet, and then the toes, and there was no more for it to do. The muscle continued, covering the ankle, tendons snapping into place, protecting the feet, and then the toes. The skin was last, and it formed.

Minutes passed, the operating room dead quiet, and Tommy healed.

The skin finished healing, and Tommy was whole again. Tears poured down Jon's cheeks, but he didn't wipe them. He did his best to blink his eyes clear. The room stayed silent. They knew the true test.

"Stop the pump," said Jon. The pump slowed to a halt. "Pull him from the nutrient bath."

The team grabbed him, needing a couple more now that he had the extra weight of legs. They guided him back to the stretcher, toweled him dry, and covered him with a sheet.

"Wake—wake him up," said Jon, his voice catching in his throat. The anesthesiologist pulled the mask off Tommy's mouth and nose. He breathed real air again, and a few minutes later, his eyes fluttered open. Jon stood there, and Tommy came back.

"Dad?" asked Tommy.

"Tommy," said Jon. He grabbed his hand. "Take it slow. Breathe for me."

Tommy breathed.

"How do you feel?" asked Jon.

"I—I can feel my toes again," said Tommy. He raised his leg and poked out his foot. "They're real." Jon hugged him then, hugged him hard. The team cheered. They had succeeded.

"Bravo! Bravo!" yelled Shaw from above.

Jon held Tommy, hugging him hard. He didn't look up to Shaw.

But he hadn't forgotten his rage.

26

Tommy took tentative steps across their living room. An old game show played on the television behind him, the volume down low. Tommy made it across the room, and then put a hand on a chair, bracing himself.

"How do they feel?" asked Jon.

"It's weird," said Tommy. "It's really weird. It's getting easier."

Jon looked at the bare legs of his son. They seemed healthy, with strong muscle, no sign of atrophy or weakness. They regenerated just as if Tommy had lost them yesterday, not six years ago. And while the legs themselves were strong, the rest of Tommy's body hadn't had lower legs for quite a while.

They had been under house arrest for a day now, with

Shaw being true to his word. The doctors had taken Tommy aside after the operation, doing every kind of test they could think of. Their prognosis is that he was as healthy as a horse. But then Shaw had talked to him.

"We don't have much time, Jon," said Shaw. "I wasn't lying about that. But everything is falling into place. Soon, we'll all be out of here, and everything will work out. Don't worry, I'll take care of you back on the surface. Regardless of our differences down here, I couldn't have done any of this without you. I will reward you, after I take control. I want to thank you, Jon. None of this would have happened without you."

And then the guards took Jon and Tommy back to their home. Jon had been wrong, because Tommy rode his wheelchair back, his balance still not good enough to walk. But after a day of practicing, he was better, almost normal. Tommy sat down again after another circuit of the living room.

"What's going to happen to us?" asked Tommy.

"I don't know," said Jon. "We're very comfortable prisoners right now. Shaw said he'll take care of us, after everything is through. I don't trust him, so who knows."

"What is Mr. Shaw planning?" asked Tommy.

"I don't know for sure," said Jon. "Tabby saw a completed beam weapon of some kind. Something powerful, very advanced. There's my research. There are dozens of other projects, and Shaw alluded to most of them being complete. He talked about factories, on the surface. My guess is he's going to try and seize power."

"He's going to take over the world?" asked Tommy. "Doesn't he already have everything he wants?"

Jon laughed. "Men like Shaw, they'll never be happy. The

only happiness they feel is fleeting, when they get what they want, but then they have to find something else they have to have. Whether it be power, or money, or even their arm back. I don't know if Shaw wants the world. Maybe he just wants a small part of it. Or to sell it to the highest bidder. But he already has all the money in the world, so I don't think it's that. I think he's going to use it to take over somewhere."

"Do you think he will?" asked Tommy.

"I don't know," said Jon. "What do you think?"

"I don't know," said Tommy. "Won't the other governments try and stop him?"

"Probably," said Jon. "But a lot of places were in shambles before we came down here. Who knows how they're doing now. They might have lost control. And that's when it's easiest for someone to step in and take it. Especially if they have the resources Shaw does."

"What can we do?" asked Tommy.

"I don't know," said Jon. "Not much, I guess. We can be frustrated. Are you okay?"

"I guess," said Tommy. "Everything worked out, I guess. I've got my legs back."

"Yeah," said Jon, exhaling. "It wasn't exactly an ideal situation, though. And I haven't forgiven Shaw."

"Isn't this what you wanted, though?" asked Tommy.

"I thought so," said Jon. "For a long time. And I'm glad you can walk again. But you were right the whole time. I made a mistake, that night, and it hurt you. But hurting you more trying to reclaim something wasn't worth it, even if it resulted in this. Your mom and I might still be together, and we'd be in a different place. Would the world be better? No. But I'm sorry, Tommy. I'm sorry for everything."

"It's okay," said Tommy, and he hugged Jon. Jon hugged him back.

"What do we do now?" asked Tommy. "Do we just wait?"

Jon sighed. His frustration, his anger and rage toward Shaw hadn't disappeared, but it was impotent now. They were trapped.

"We wait," said Jon. "We watch some old TV shows. Hope for the best, I guess."

"Can I play a game?" asked Tommy.

"Sure," said Jon. "I'll be reading in my room if you need me."

Tommy set up a game on the big screen, and Jon went back to his bedroom, laying down and opening up his tablet. The ShawNet had a huge eBook library, and he had all the time in the world to read. He started Anna Karenina when his phone buzzed on the nightstand.

He looked at it. They had turned off messaging and calls for him, for everyone in house arrest. He had tried to contact Tabby a thousand times, but it never worked. The phone buzzed again, and Jon grabbed it. It simply read Operations. Maybe they were calling to ask for a grocery order. He answered.

"Hello?" said Jon.

"Hello, Dr. Matthews," said a familiar voice. "This is Nadia."

"Um, hello," said Jon. "I—I didn't expect you to call me."

"No, I imagine not," said Nadia. "I have a proposition for you, Dr. Matthews."

"Please, just call me Jon," he said. "And what is it? Is this another of Shaw's deals?"

"I don't work for Shaw," said Nadia.

"I—what?" asked Jon. "Yes, you do."

"My proposition is this. I get you out from house arrest, along with your son, and anyone else you need. I get you to the surface, and I take you to safety, provided you fulfill your end of the bargain."

"And what is that?" asked Jon.

"You kill Eaton Shaw," said Nadia. "In roughly three hours, Shaw will undergo the same procedure as Tommy, to re-grow his arm. Dr. Stone will oversee it. It provides us with an opportunity, a very rare opportunity, where Shaw will be vulnerable. And you're uniquely qualified to help, with your knowledge."

Jon sat quietly, and Nadia didn't interrupt it. Jon finally spoke. "Before I give you an answer, can I ask a few questions?"

"Ask away," said Nadia.

"Why do you want Shaw dead?"

"Because he's a warlord oligarch who has enslaved a large part of the world, and he means to take control of an even larger part of the Earth, using technology harvested in the FUTURE lab. Not to mention the many minor transgressions he's committed, for example, using your son as a guinea pig for a procedure he's undergoing himself."

"Then who do you work for, if it's not for Shaw?"

"I'm a part of an underground group, trying to save the world. Or at least slightly improve it."

"So you have access to the surface?"

"Yes," said Nadia.

"Is everything okay up there?"

"Well, no. But things are better than Shaw has let on. Dr. Knight was correct in her estimation. There was no nuclear attack. There is still minor unrest, bordering on major in certain areas, but nothing cataclysmic, yet. Shaw's movement will trigger it, though. And we're almost certain that's by design."

"Do you know how Maya's doing? Tommy's mom?"

"She's surviving," said Nadia. "I have access to all the information Shaw does. Aside from his most private files, but even those aren't impregnable."

"Where are we?"

"You're roughly a mile under the southern tip of Greenland," said Nadia.

"Jesus," said Jon. "I guess getting to the surface wouldn't get us anywhere."

"No," said Nadia. "Not without transport. But I can arrange that. We have a chopper in Iceland."

"Why me?" asked Jon.

"Why you what?"

"Why am I the one to do it?" asked Jon. "To kill Shaw."

"Because you're personally motivated. You have intimate knowledge of the procedure, and can insert failure points at numerous places, provided support. And frankly, all our other operatives down here have failed."

"How many are there?" asked Jon.

"There were a half dozen," said Nadia. "Including me. But I'm the only one left. Shaw is smart, and pays attention, and doesn't sleep. And one by one, he ferreted them out."

"Did he—"

"Kill them?" asked Nadia. "Yes."

"I guess I shouldn't be surprised," said Jon. "How do I know you're telling me the truth?"

"You don't," said Nadia. "I could be representing any

kind of interest. Shaw has many enemies. But I'm *not* lying. I need your help. Shaw makes sure to limit his vulnerabilities. This will be our last chance."

"Aren't I safer just staying in my room and not doing anything?"

"Most likely. I do believe Shaw will take care of you when this is all over, if he wins. Our guess is that he will win, if we don't stop him now. We can't compete with his resources." She paused. "But it's not the right thing to do. From my time watching you, you seem to value that."

"Will killing Shaw really stop his machine? Won't someone take his place?"

"We have teams across the world in place to take out his lieutenants, so to speak," said Nadia. "Other stockholders, and people instrumental to him. But we're waiting for him to fall first. Without him, and without them, it will fall apart."

"What will happen to everyone else down here?"

"We'll do our best to extract them as well," said Nadia.

A million thoughts flew through Jon's mind. About his role in this. About Tommy. About his safety, and the thought of the whole world. He remembered Tabby's response to the weapon, of its power. Of Shaw's face watching the mutated chimp absorbing guards.

He would do that on a massive scale. Imagine a wave of those things spreading through a city. There'd be nothing left but them.

"Say I agree to your plan," said Jon. "Aren't there a bunch of guards, and a bunch of other systems in place that will stop me?"

"All systems have weak points," said Nadia. "Shaw insisted a human operate all his door, security, and camera systems. He didn't trust an AI, thinking it could be hacked, making it vulnerable. And to a certain extent, he's correct. But unfortunately for him, he chose me. There will be guards, down near the operating theater and close to Shaw. Nothing I can do about that. But otherwise, I control everything. I can get you right there."

"Then I agree," said Jon. "I want Tabby and Mel freed, too."

"Done," said Nadia. "You can collect them on the way. I would advise bringing Tommy with you, as well."

"Isn't he safer here?" asked Jon. "You can control who gets in and out."

"It's possible he's safer there," said Nadia. "But this plan is not perfect. It has multiple points of failure, and any of them could result in Shaw leveraging Tommy against you. And frankly, I can control access to a lot of places, but there are mechanical means to get anywhere in here, with the right knowledge. Those doors can't hold up to shotgun blasts."

Jon, Tommy, and Mel appeared at Tabby's door twenty minutes later. Tabby hugged Jon hard, before noticing that Tommy was walking.

"Holy shit," said Tabby. "You have legs."

"I'm still a little wobbly," said Tommy.

"What's going on, Jon?" asked Tabby. "I've been in the dark for weeks."

Jon thought for a moment. "Shaw wants his arm back. We're going to stop him."

27

Nadia hadn't lied, because she had cleared the way. Jon explained it as they went, and none of them objected. They all wanted to stop Shaw.

The hallways of the residential area were quiet. They always were, but there was no one out. Most were under house arrest. Shaw had used them for their purpose, and then stored them for later, just in case.

Back in the elevator.

"What's the plan?" asked Tabby.

"With Nadia's help, we create a CRISPR scrambler, just like we did for the mutated chimp," said Jon. "We disguise as surgical assistants, get close during the operation, and inject Shaw."

"That'll kill him," said Mel.

"Yes, it will," said Jon. The thought had crossed his mind that they were more than just stopping him. This was an assassination. Jon largely was a pacifist, but Shaw—Shaw was trying to take over the world. He had killed many. And Tommy could have easily died in the test. So Jon pushed the idea aside. "At this point, that's what it will take."

Mel said nothing, only nodded, but Jon could see the discomfort in her face. In the end, he would pull the trigger, if it came to it.

"Our equipment is still there, in the medical pillar, away from the dark lab. We prepare there, sneak down into the dark lab, join the operation as quietly as possible, and inject Shaw."

"Sounds like a plan," said Tabby. "How much of that was you, Nadia?"

"Half," said Nadia, from around them. The elevator moved then, quickly, stopping at the medical pillar. The elevator opened up, and Jon remembered his first stop here, months ago, seeing the place for the first time. And the last, after the success with the rats.

It was empty now, abandoned. Everyone had either moved up or moved out, and it was eerie, the lights on but no one home. Every step echoed, and every lab was open, all the glass clear. Jon had never seen it like this.

They beelined to their old lab.

"It seemed so big back then," said Mel, moving to her workstation.

Mel turned everything on, logging into the ShawNet. Jon leaned over her shoulder. Tabby and Tommy waited nearby.

"We'll provide moral support," said Tabby.

"You're an extra sets of hands," said Jon. "In case we need

them. I feel better having you around. *And*—you're the only who's seen that energy weapon handled."

Mel typed furiously, her hands skating around the keyboard. Windows popped up and closed.

"I'm opening up the CRISPR software," said Mel. "I'll tell it to make the scrambler."

"Tell it to make two," said Jon. "Just in case."

Mel typed some more.

"Goddamnit," she muttered.

"What's wrong?" asked Jon.

"It's not processed," said Mel. "It's been too long. The system emptied it out. Stone's been messing around in here since he's been in charge."

"Well, how long would it take?" asked Jon.

"A couple hours," said Mel.

"We don't have the time," said Tabby.

"What can we make?" asked Jon. "What formulas are already processed?"

"There's three. The zero formula. The one used on Tommy, and presumably also on Shaw," said Mel. "And the one we used on the chimp that went berserk."

Jon sighed. "Make that one, then. Two copies."

"The berserk formula? It wasn't prepped for humans, and that thing—"

"It's all we have," said Jon. "It'll disrupt his systems, regardless. We'll just have to be ready to run."

"If you say so," said Mel, and started the system, the computer doing all the hard stuff, pairing the complex mix of material necessary for the CRISPR to work.

Within minutes, the first and then second copies of the serum were ready, only needed to be injected to perform their magic.

"Now the difficult part," said Jon.

"You're clear for everywhere but the operating theater and the armory," said Nadia. "And anyone with camera feeds won't see you. I've looped old footage of nothing. They think everyone is locked up, so they're not being particularly vigilant. I'll warn you if you're in danger of being seen. There are surgical scrubs in your first lab in the dark lab. You ready?"

"Yes," said Jon, after glances around, and the elevator plunged down. Moments later, the dark lab lay in front of them. Jon led them in, glancing around, but seeing and hearing nothing. They followed him to their first lab down there, now emptied of most stuff. Jon went to the supply closet and opened boxes, pulling out surgical scrubs, enough for all of them to wear. His phone buzzed in his pocket.

"Nadia," he answered.

"They will start the pre-op routine in ten minutes," she said. "Two assistants, roughly matching the sizes and shapes of you and Dr. Underwood are locked in their rooms. You should be able to step in as them without raising eyebrows, as long as you don't talk too much and don't let people see you."

"Understood," said Jon. "Their names."

"Steven Bollard. Barbara Tyler. Also goes by Babs."

"Got it," said Jon, and Nadia hung up.

"We all dress up," said Jon, throwing the scrubs to all of them. "But only Mel and I go in with Shaw and rest of them. I'm Steven Bollard. Mel, you're Barbara Tyler, also called Babs. Tabby, Tommy, you will hang back, and be backup in case we need it. Tabby, try and access the energy weapon."

"It's under lock and key," said Tabby. "Nadia said the armory is guarded."

"Whenever we stick Shaw," said Jon. "Things are going to get messy, quickly. So be ready. I'll message you, but I don't think I'll need to."

Everyone was dressed, mostly covered in scrubs. Jon had worked to cover up most of his face. They all did. Tommy, with his legs, looked like a short adult. The bluff would work for a moment, at least.

"Everyone ready?" asked Jon. They all nodded. Jon hugged Tommy and Tabby. "Good luck."

They went their separate ways, and Jon didn't look back, saying goodbye to his son again, heading directly into the lion's den. He could have stayed in his room, and avoided all of this, but that would be letting this monster do what he pleased. That thought clicked in him. He remembered Shaw's words. "I wouldn't have been able to do this without you." Jon had helped build this, and now he would destroy it.

Jon and Mel walked toward the operating theater in the corner of the dark lab. He expected guards soon, but they didn't blink when he saw the two approach.

"Jesus, they've been waiting on you two," said a guard, one of four standing around outside the door. The two of them walked in. Jon had a knot of anxiety in his stomach, and tried to push it away, to act natural. He was Steven Bollard. He was running late, he was nervous, but he wasn't planning anything untoward. He felt the serum in his pocket.

Everyone stared at them as they entered, and Jon's heart froze. They were all the in the pre-op room, getting ready.

Most just glanced, but they all looked, and one of them would realize who they were. But no one did.

"Where the hell have you two been?" asked the loud voice of Stone, who was washing up under a sink.

"Our alarm didn't go off," said Mel, her voice higher than normal. Jon hoped she had met Babs.

Stone glanced at them a moment longer, across the room. "Really? You two? Well, okay. Get ready for the operation. Bollard, you're on the pump. Tyler, you're assisting the anesthesiologist. No different from Jon's kid. Same procedure. You're lucky Shaw's not here yet. He'd rip your ass apart."

Jon and Mel glanced at each other and then played their parts, getting ready for the procedure, just like they would on a normal day, trying to keep their heads down and faces hidden. Only answering questions when necessary.

But no one spoke. They were operating on Shaw today, and Jon doubted Shaw hadn't read them the riot act. And only a few minutes passed before Shaw came in, covered in a surgical gown, not wearing his prosthetic. Jon knew not to look, but he had never seen Shaw without it, and he looked odd, naked. Shaw protected his image like he everything else he owned, and Jon understood why Shaw had waited until he would have his arm again before he went back to the surface.

It was a symbol, the ultimate representation of power. Shaw could do anything, including miracles. He had the power of God, and he would exercise it.

Jon turned his head back, busying himself with the nutrient pump. It was ready to go, but he examined it, back and forth, endlessly. Two guards flanked Shaw, each armed with an assault rifle.

"Please, Mr. Shaw," said Stone. "This is a clean room, we can't have—"

"I decide what kind of room this is, Doctor," said Shaw. "And if you expect me to not have my guards, you're sorely mistaken. Also, I've decided that I will not be put under anesthesia for the procedure."

"What?" asked Stone. "I don't think that's a good idea, sir. We do not know what kind of pain the regeneration process causes. Even reopening the wound site will be quite painful, and your response—"

"I was awake when it was removed the first time, Dr. Stone," said Shaw. "I'll be awake the second. I can't go under. Too many variables."

Jon cursed under his breath. Another set of eyes studying them, looking for sabotage. Jon felt the serum in his pocket again, making sure it was there.

"Okay," said Stone. "But it will hurt, a lot."

"I will manage," said Shaw.

"Lay down on the stretcher," said Stone. "We're going to clean the wound site, and then get you into the theater."

Shaw complied, and one of the assistants scrubbed his stump, cleaning it for surgery.

"Alright, let's move him," said Stone, to the assembled team. Jon grabbed the vacuum pump. A massive tub of nutrient bath was already in the theater, too heavy to be moved by hand. They carried Shaw in and set him down, with the same procedure as Tommy. But no sedative this time. Shaw would be awake when they cut into him.

Jon kept eyes off of him, as much as possible. It wasn't hard, as everyone milled around, doing their duty, all of them dressed the same. This was the easy part. Situating himself so he could inject Shaw instead of Stone would be the hard part. He eyed Mel, and he could tell she was thinking the same thing.

Jon looked to Mel again, trying to communicate with only his eyes, but she was turned. She had no anesthesiologist to assist, so she busied herself with the container for the bathtub that they would immerse Shaw in. But his heart leapt into his throat. Her hair dangled from underneath her surgical cap. Just a few strands. But her hair was dark, raven colored, and he didn't know what Bab's hair color was. He hoped it was black. He couldn't say anything, not now. Shaw's eyes wondered in his direction and he bent down, his face out of sight. Shaw would recognize him in an instant if he let him.

"Are we ready?" asked Shaw. "I don't have all day."

"Yes, Mr. Shaw," said Stone. "I think we're ready."

"Great," said Shaw. "The floor is yours, Doctor." Shaw took a deep breath. Jon wondered if he was nervous. Did Shaw even get nervous? Jon didn't know, but he doubted it. Shaw seemed to have infinite confidence, built from a lifetime of always being lucky, of things always going his way.

Except for his arm. And now he was going to rectify that.

Not if Jon could help it.

"There won't be anesthesia," said Stone. "So let's begin by re-opening the wound site. Will, go ahead."

The surgeon looked to Shaw, who nodded at him, and he cut, little by little, slicing away the skin that had been shaped around the raw muscle and bone after Shaw's accident. Shaw grunted and gritted his teeth, but he didn't flinch, even as the blood poured from his arm. His vitals were all over the place, his heart rate soaring. But the surgeon continued to work. They vacuumed and wiped away the blood, and soon the wound was re-opened.

"Move him to the tub," said Stone, but they didn't need to carry Shaw, only assist him off the stretcher, into the tub, blood spurting out of his arm. He sunk into the tub, his arm sticking out.

We have to do it now. Stone will inject him next. He looked to Mel, and she met his eyes. Even more of her hair was revealed. But Mel was getting closer to Shaw now. Jon inched his way there, but he had to stay within reach of the pump. He eyed Stone, who had the syringe in his hand.

"Preparing to inject—"

But then he stopped. He was staring at Mel.

"Take off your mask," he said, his voice loud.

"Who? Me?" asked Mel.

"Yes," said Stone.

"What are you doing, Doctor?" asked Shaw.

"I—" started Mel, but Stone walked to her in a quick motion, and ripped it off, revealing her face.

"We have an intruder," said Stone. "Jon's assistant."

"Get her out of here!" yelled Shaw, but Jon saw his chance with Stone out of the way. He quickly inserted the serum into a syringe, stepped up and injected Shaw in his shoulder.

"Don't worry, Mr. Shaw. You'll look *beautiful*," said Jon, into his ear. The guards converged on Mel, grabbing her, but Shaw was yelling, yelling already.

Stone, it's Dr. Matthe—" Shaw yelled, but the serum did its work. His arm grew, his body drinking in the nutrient bath, but Jon didn't turn on the pump. Jon grabbed a medical tray from nearby and ran to a guard, swinging it as hard as he could. The guard wore a helmet, but it still knocked him silly, leaving a single man holding Mel.

He raised his rifle, but then Shaw made a noise, a guttural moan, loud, filling the room, and his arm began to mutate.

28

Shaw's arm mutated quickly, and Shaw only screamed and grunted as his flesh grew and mutated.

"Please, more!" he screamed, and Jon didn't know what he meant, but his arm continued to grow, the bone and muscle intertwining, just like the rats, just like the chimps.

Everyone stared in horror, doing nothing. Shaw climbed out of the tub awkwardly, grabbing the edge with his still growing arm, and then plunged it through the plastic coating of the hundred gallon container that held the nutrient bath. It spilled out, coating the limb, and it grew, the liquid soaking into Shaw's skin. The arm grew faster then, as fast as Shaw's body could take, and it became larger and larger.

Shaw's body pulsated, shining as it bloated, Jon able to see the pulse of the mutation as it spread through his frame.

"More!" yelled Shaw. "I need more!" The words came from deep in his gut, and Jon barely understood him. The heavy container of liquid was emptying fast. Within a minute it would be gone. Still, it only lingered at the bottom of the tank, and Shaw couldn't reach it.

He turned to face the assembled team, a dozen of them, plus the two guards. Shaw screamed again, and his body distended, his legs and other arm contorting, twisting, the skin bursting, reforming, bursting again, muscle splitting it wide open, strips of bone and cartilage interlaced. Shaw could only scream.

Stone was the first to speak.

"Shoot him!" he yelled at the guards, and the guards turned to him, forgetting Jon and Mel. Shaw whipped over a massive still mutating arm, hitting Stone with a thick thud in his chest, a horrible SNAP filling the room. Stone flew into the corner, smashing through piles of equipment. He softly groaned.

The guards opened fire then, full auto with their assault rifles, and Jon dove to the ground, pulling Mel with him. The gunfire was deafening inside the room, and dozens of rounds spit out from the rifles. They peppered Shaw, sick thuds with splatters of blood and gore. A few of the rounds missed, a couple members of the team falling to the bullets.

Shaw screamed as the weapons clicked empty, and the guards reached for more clips. Jon scrambled to his feet and pulled Mel with him, away from the troops as Shaw charged them, leaking from dozens of bullet wounds. But they were healing, fissures closing in his skin, more flesh being generated, more muscle being built, every wound only strengthening him. His face was the only thing left that looked human, but even now it was changing, his chin and nose and eyebrows growing, bone thickening.

Shaw charged the guards, and grabbed each of them in each arm, entangling them in flesh, sticking to them, tendrils of slimy skin absorbing them, their mass becoming Shaw's. They screamed until they had no tongues.

Shaw turned, each of the guards still in his hands, when the doors flew open, the four guards outside, investigating the gunfire. The rest of the team had fled, and Jon and Mel dove again, out of the way of the additional guards. They opened fire, three with assault rifles, but the last had a flamethrower, and he waited for the three others to fire. Ninety rounds hit Shaw in center mass, digging a blood furrow into his torso. But he only healed, absorbing quickly from the two guards, the limp remnants of their bodies hanging loosely from his arms, what remained of them sluicing through their clothes.

But it slowed him down, and the noise Shaw made showed he still felt pain, a mastodon roar of agony and suffering. Hot shell casings tumbled on and around Jon. He heard a soft moaning as the gunfire ceased and saw Stone lying against the wall. Blood poured from his mouth and nose. Shaw had crushed something inside of him.

"J—Jon," he sputtered. The flamethrower had stepped up, a bright blue flame ready to shoot.

Stone crawled to him and grabbed his hand as the flames filled the room with immense heat. Jon turned to look as the inferno engulfed Shaw, and the creature screamed again, its new flesh burning, blistering, charring, and then sloughing off, new meat already underneath. The flamethrower advanced, and Shaw actually retreated, trying to fall away from the incredible heat, the pain of being roasted alive.

"The sc—scrambler," said Stone. "Last one. My desk drawer." Stone stared at him, but his eyes were still, dead. Jon opened his hand to reveal a key. Shaw screamed again, a terrifying yell of something unheard on Earth before. The flamethrower shot fire, a burning arc of liquid flame that doused Shaw, and it was working. Shaw regenerated, but he couldn't regrow tissue faster than it burned. Shaw had retreated back near the massive nutrient tub. He leaned into it, ripping open the hole he had pierced earlier, and pushed his way inside, diving into the bottom of the container.

"We need to go, now!" said Jon, pulling Mel to her feet, sprinting. The flamethrower still shot, but Shaw was underneath the surface of the liquid, bubbles coming up. Jon stumbled to his feet, Mel beside him, and he turned to see Shaw emerge soaked in the nutrient bath, flying through the hole, straight through the gout of flames, and mounting the body of the guard who wielded the flamethrower. The flames stopped, and Shaw had healed, the milky white liquid putting out the fire and giving him food, and now the guard gave him more, Shaw's torso absorbing the man, both his arms extending out, giant masses of flesh whipping into two of the three remaining guards and pulling them in.

Jon sprinted, with Mel beside him, out of the operating room, into the pre-op room, and then out the door. The fourth guard ran beside them, directly into a squad of twelve guards, armed with shotguns and two more flamethrowers.

"It's another one of those things!" yelled the guard. Jon pointed inside, and the dozen men lined up outside, giving them a choke point.

A massive roar erupted from inside, a thudding bass

note.

"Was that a word?" asked Mel.

"Yeah. He said my name," said Jon. "We need to get to Stone's office." They ran, as Shaw emerged from the operating theater, bursting out into the corridor, and the squad opened fire, shotgun blasts and two flamethrowers, on full blast. Jon didn't turn to see the results, but heard the chaos behind him. Ultimately, he heard death.

Shaw had learned from his experience with the first flamethrowers, and Jon didn't need to look to hear the sound of first, and then the second weapon extinguish, the familiar *whoosh* disappearing, men screaming as Shaw engulfed them. They ran, turning the corner, with the sounds of shotguns still filling the level. But they quieted, one by one.

"JON," shouted the Shaw creature, and there were no more sounds of shotgun blasts, and Jon looked now as they sprinted toward Stone's office. The Shaw creature loped after them. It still grew, absorbing the squad that had attacked it. Parts of it burned, but soon the mass of flesh engulfed the flame. Jon saw the arms and legs of guards sticking out from the mass, now on all fours, running like a gorilla, its flesh skidding along the ground, the only thing slowing it.

Jon sprinted hard, turning a corner, and then another, Mel beside him.

"Go, find Tabby," said Jon. She nodded and split off. The creature only wanted him, the fragment of mind that was still Shaw knowing deep down that Jon had done this to him. Jon heard crashing behind him, and he glanced to see the great behemoth smash through the black glass walls of the different labs, not bothering to take corners anymore, following Jon, dead set to kill him, to absorb him, to make him one with the mass.

Jon felt something whip by him, and a glass tile flew by his head, smashing into pieces on the ground. He looked and the Shaw creature grabbed them as it ran, flinging them like a lacrosse player at Jon. He ducked, a massive tile flying by him, fast enough to decapitate.

"JON," yelled the thing, now ten feet tall and just as wide, Jon only barely able to recognize limbs and torso. Any remnants of the guards were visible only by the remains of their uniforms, pieces of black cloth and kevlar dotting the outside of the creature. Still, it grew. He could see its flesh bubbling up, expanding. Its great blubber bounced off the ground, and soon it wasn't running, but more rolling, moving like a worm, pushing itself in massive leaps. Jon ran. There was nothing left that could stop it now, except for the scrambler.

He hoped. It had worked on the mutated chimp, but the Shaw thing was now over twice the size of that, and still growing. Would it have an effect? Jon didn't know, but he hoped it would. He didn't know how else to stop whatever Shaw had become.

It only wanted to feed and grow. That's what they had programmed it to do, to only generate, to make more of itself, more flesh, more mass. Driven by Shaw's instincts, it chased after Jon.

And it was gaining. Jon sprinted as hard as he could, and Stone's office was near, less than a minute away. But he didn't know if he'd make it that far. He didn't dare look, not now, but he felt the thing behind him, glass crashing and whizzing by him, a buzz saw of flesh and bone ready to eat him alive.

Then he saw the lab, their old lab, attached to the smaller operating theater, rebuilt after the chimp, and Jon found a reserve he didn't know he had, running harder. He was going to make it. He was going to stop this thing and kill Shaw for good.

But then his feet were taken out from underneath him, and he flew, tumbling as he hit the ground, sliding along the glass, a sharp pain in his shoulder, and he grunted as he rolled along. He slammed into a glass wall. The creature had swiped out and caught a foot, and he had tumbled ass over teakettle.

He couldn't move his left arm. It was dislocated.

"JON," said the thing again, and it was right there, almost on top of him. It had slowed, and it was just a worm now, its legs and arms only small tendrils, four of dozens extending out from its mass. Jon didn't know what Shaw would become, given enough time, but it leaked blood and bile from dozens of orifices, opening and closing as the creature burst from the pressure within. Shaw's eyes stared out from the middle of it, his head gone, the only thing left that was still him. Maybe Shaw still thought, maybe his mind and self were still contained within, but the eyes were the only evidence, dark amber, looking. They studied him, tendrils of red, beige, and white flesh reaching toward him.

Jon held his breath, waiting for the end.

"Jon, close your eyes!" yelled Tabby, and Jon did.

There was a click, and a bright flash, and a sudden splash.

Jon opened his eyes, and a third of the creature had been turned into liquid gore, splattering the walls and floor, a puddle of the Shaw abomination.

It emitted a great noise of pain and turned toward Tabby.

29

Tabby, flanked by Tommy and Mel, carried the energy weapon in her arms. It was small, smaller than the assault rifles the guards carried, a contoured rectangle of metal with a stock and trigger attached. A narrow aperture on its face shot out plasma death.

The creature screamed, a third of its mass now liquid on the floor. It surged toward her, recognizing the threat.

"Get the shot!" yelled Tabby, and fired again. Jon averted his eyes with the click, and light filled the room, and more of the mass disappeared, destroyed by the powerful energy weapon. But it still was huge, dwarfing all of them. The carved paths where the weapon had hit it had cauterized, scorched black and smoking. The smell hit Jon, and he held back vomit.

But Shaw wasn't healing where the weapon hit it. The mass still bubbled up from inside, expanding and growing elsewhere, but not where the weapon scorched it. Jon scrambled to his feet, his left arm dangling uselessly, and he sprinted away from the creature back toward the lab.

The creature was torn, but moved quickly toward Tabby, only thirty feet away from her. She fired again, the loud CLICK filling the room, and Jon wasn't looking now. He saw the light in front of him and heard the weapon discharge, like the sound of a Polaroid camera.

He ran to Stone's desk, unlocked it, and found the shot, just rolling around on top. Stone had kept one around, just in case. He knew better than to trust Shaw.

Jon heard Tabby fire another shot, and another flash of light filtered into the lab. How could Shaw still be alive? Maybe they wouldn't need the shot at all. Jon ran back out.

Tabby had cut Shaw down to size, the blasts from the energy weapon obliterating parts of the great thing. Huge swathes of flesh had been melted off it, with lines of black char all over its body. But Jon still saw Shaw's eyes. Wherever the intelligence in this thing was, Tabby had not extinguished it.

"Aim for his eyes!" yelled Jon. Tabby heard him, nodded, and pulled the rifle. She aimed and squeezed the trigger. Jon closed his eyes. But there was no CLICK, and no light, and no sound of a Polaroid camera going off. Jon opened his eyes.

Tabby looked at the gun, confused.

Jon's heart sank. She was out of juice, clear she didn't have any extra batteries. The creature had slunk back, waiting for the shot of pain, but it never came, and its posture changed. It slithered backward.

What is it doing?

But then Jon saw. The great mass of meat had sunk itself into the ruined puddle of its old flesh. Melted off of it in a sudden blast of energy. But it was still useful, and the terrible thing absorbed it, pulling the old parts of it back in, feeding and growing.

"Oh no," said Jon. The creature grew again, reconstructing not through its blackened wounds, but around them, pushing the scar tissue deep inside, adjusting to its new body. Because there was no destroying this. It would only regenerate.

Jon squeezed the scrambler serum in his fist. It would kill it, but he couldn't get close enough to give it the shot. Shaw would obliterate him if he got within ten feet, tendrils whipping through the air. He needed a tranq gun.

The Shaw monster grew again, nearly at its original size, building back its strength. Jon ran to Tabby.

"I need a tranq gun!" yelled Jon.

"The armory," said Tabby, and they all ran, not looking back at the massive creature. It screamed again.

"JON," it yelled, lungs still somewhere inside of it, a bellow filling the dark lab. They ran, passing a squad of soldiers, with more shotguns and flamethrowers.

"Don't!" yelled Jon as they passed, but they ignored him. They had orders, orders to fight the thing, and die as it ate them. Shaw would only grow larger as they fed more meat into the grinder.

They ran for the armory, passing more men running the other way. The floor shook now with the tremor of the great beast, as thousands of pounds of growing mass thumped along the floor, slithering on its own blood and bile, leaving a trail like a slug.

It followed them, still, followed *him*, still. It wanted to kill him, to eat him, to absorb him. The guards would all die, but they slowed down the creature, slowed it down long enough for them to reach the armory without problem. The sounds of shotgun blasts and assault rifles and flamethrowers all stopped, but they were inside, empty now, all the men now gone to feed the beast.

Tabby pointed, and Jon saw them. A row of tranq rifles, unused, and Jon grabbed one and loaded the serum inside. He couldn't miss.

"It's coming," said Jon, the armory shaking, and then the world exploded, the creature smashing through the walls, sending glass and shelves and metal flying everywhere. They all tumbled, and the rifle flew out of Jon's hands. He rolled, something opening up his head as he flew.

Jon stopped and opened his eyes. The great mass of the creature stood there, pulsating. He found Shaw's eyes on the beast, and they looked at him, waiting for him. It again had paused when it could have enveloped him easily. It hadn't. Jon met the gaze of Shaw's eyes, and he realized that this Shaw thing wanted him to know his end was coming. Jon looked around, located Tommy, Mel, and Tabby scattered around the room. All of them shook their heads, trying to collect themselves.

And then Jon saw Shaw's eyes move off of him and look elsewhere.

"TOMMY," it bellowed, a dark, booming noise. It charged toward Tommy. It would punish Jon.

No

Jon spotted the rifle, a few feet away on the ground, and dove toward it. He grabbed it, his shoulder screaming with pain, but he held it and fired it at the great beast.

THUNK

The rifle fired, a thin stream of gas emitting from the weapon, and the dart flew and stuck into the side of the monster, a small prick, a minor threat, one probably not recognized, not when its whole life had been pain.

Now Jon could only watch. It still charged at Tommy, who had gotten up on a knee, about to stand up. It moved fast for its great size, and it hit him, grabbing him with tendrils. Jon's heart sunk, and tears ran down his face.

But then the flesh of the beast sloughed away. A little at first, and then quickly, all the nature that bound its flesh together failing, all at once. It melted away, and the creature screamed again, but the noise had less force, and less, and less. Rivers of matter ran onto the ground, melted into base elements. They watched its DNA unravel before their eyes. Jon saw the eyes of Shaw then, and they saw each other, before the eyes fell away, just like the rest of it. Tommy tumbled out of the melting grasp of the thing.

Jon went to him, stepping through the puddles of flesh that surrounded them.

"Tommy!" said Jon, as he approached his son.

"Dad, I—" he started, but then Jon saw the blood. Tommy grabbed his side. Jon pulled up Tommy's shirt to reveal a puncture wound, where one of Shaw's tendrils had plunged its way inside to feed on Tommy.

"Are you okay?" asked Jon, frantically.

"I don't know, I don't know," said Tommy. "It hurts."

"Tabby, Mel, do you know where the first aid kit is?"

asked Jon. "We need doctors—"

And then Tommy screamed, a terrible scream of pain and trauma. Jon looked to Tommy and saw the flesh beneath the wound pulsate.

Tommy began to heal.

30

"Dad, what's happening?" asked Tommy.

Jon looked down at Tommy's torso, where Shaw had spiked him. Blood no longer poured from the wound, and he saw something move beneath Tommy's skin.

Oh god.

They hadn't tested the serum that regrew Tommy's legs, or the chimp's arm. They had assumed it had worked because the procedure had completed without complication, and both the chimp and Tommy had walked away.

But they hadn't thought about the rest of their lives, the rest of their lives spent with new DNA. How would their bodies react to fresh injuries? Shaw had envisioned instant healing, a future without trauma. Jon's own words echoed in his mind.

What if it gets injured again? It could trigger further mutation.

Tommy was healing the wound, but it had triggered something else, the growth of new flesh, and once it started, it wouldn't stop.

Shaw had rushed them, from formula to formula, and they had tested none of them long term. The first chimp they had healed had seemed stable. Just like Tommy had seemed stable. Jon looked at Tommy's injury and saw the healing process start anew. They had no nutrient bath, no controlled lab environment. Outside of it, the same process that had brought back his legs would start churning its way to fix the injury caused by Shaw. *But without that controlled environment—*

"Oh no, no no, no," said Jon, grabbing Tommy. His mind sped, trying to think of a solution.

There's only one, and you know it. You just gave it to Shaw.

No, Jon refused, he'd sooner die than kill Tommy. No, there had to be another way. There had to be some other fix. Tammy and Mel stared at him, confused, hopeless.

"What do we do?" asked Mel.

"Wait, wait, let me think," said Jon. Tommy squeezed his side and groaned. *They had no time, they had no time, think, Jon, think.* They needed to reset him, revert him back to—

"The zero formula," said Jon. "Remember it, Mel?"

"Yes, yes," said Mel.

Jon looked to Tommy, who moaned in pain. He was changing already. He wouldn't last much longer. "From down here, can you instruct the computer in the medical pillar to make it?"

"Yes," said Mel.

"Good," said Jon. "Do it." He looked to Tabby, and kissed her once, and then grabbed Tommy, putting his arm over his shoulder, making their way to the elevator. He had to get Tommy away from the rest of them. He'd turn soon, unable to be reasoned with, and he wouldn't have Tommy be a killer, for any reason. He knew what he had to do, clear in his mind.

He felt Tommy shake next to him.

"You with me, son?" asked Jon, as they moved toward the elevator. Jon half dragged Tommy. Jon's left arm still barely worked, and he paused a moment to slam it into a glass panel, and it slid back into place with screaming pain.

"Yeah," said Tommy, with labored breath. "It hurts so much. My insides are burning."

"Stay with me," said Jon. "Stay with me. I'll fix you, don't worry."

Tommy screamed again and felt Tommy's arm mutate. He saw the elevator, and then they were there, and Jon dragged him inside.

"The medical pillar, Nadia," said Jon. The doors closed, and then it moved. Tommy continued to mutate, his arms and legs bloating, distending. His face was still his, though, and he screamed in pain.

"I can't," said Tommy, and Jon saw the pain in his eyes. He knew what was happening inside his son. The regeneration had begun, already finished healing the wound caused by Shaw, but it wouldn't stop making more flesh, and it needed fuel, and Tommy had a limited supply. Soon it would eat away all his fat, and then muscle, a constant cycle until it was all eaten up, and Tommy would die. It was what drove the creatures, the need to fuel that engine. Jon had pulled Tommy away from the food source, all the humans left down in the dark lab.

But he wouldn't let his son starve to death, no matter what form he took. The elevator sped toward the medical pillar, and Jon took his son's arm and put it around him, and Tommy fed on him. Jon felt it, and the pain of his flesh being siphoned away nearly pushed him into unconsciousness.

But he pulled himself back, he had to, otherwise they would both die for nothing. Tommy screamed again, but he wouldn't starve, pulling flesh away from Jon. Jon felt himself being absorbed, but they had enough time. They had to.

The elevator doors opened.

"Good luck, Doctor," said Nadia, and Jon pulled Tommy, now together as one. Jon's legs didn't want to work, but he made them work, he forced them forward, his old lab not that far away, only a few hundred feet. He could make it. He would fix Tommy, he would finish what he started, he would correct his mistake.

Step after step on clear glass tiles, lit with white light. Blood trailed behind them as Tommy continued to mutate, his torso distending now, his legs and arms thickening, engorging. He moaned in pain.

"You still with me, son?" asked Jon, but Tommy only grunted now. The mutation was taking over. Jon felt himself losing strength, what reserves he had being siphoned away. But he would finish this.

He could see his lab now, fifty feet away. His feet didn't want to work, he couldn't feel them anymore, but he looked down at them, and made them move, didn't look at what Tommy was doing to him, wouldn't have his last memory of his son be this. If he would die, he would remember Tommy as a boy, not this thing.

But they were at the lab now, the doors open. Jon only had a single arm and leg now and he grabbed and clawed his way to the workstation, where the CRISPR software worked. The serum sat there, in the machine, ready. He dragged the squalling mess that was his son and what remained of himself over to it. He couldn't breathe, a bloody mess of air choking in his throat, but he had the strength for this.

Jon grabbed the serum and slid it with shaking fingers into a syringe, and popped off the safety lid with his teeth, Tommy pulling more and more of him inside.

"Don't worry, son," said Jon. "I'll fix you."

He plunged the needle into the growing mass that was Tommy, which screamed and moaned now as it grew. His strength was fading. He dropped the needle now. Soon he would be gone.

But then Tommy changed, the mass receding, falling off, sloughing off just like Shaw had done, and Jon felt the thing that Tommy had become let loose of him, let loose of whatever was left, as the extraneous flesh melted away, undone by the serum. Jon fell to the floor, and Tommy groaned in pain, shaking, more and more of his extra flesh falling away, until only he remained. He slumped to the floor, his new legs gone again.

He collapsed next to Jon, breathing hard, wet and slimy, like from the womb.

"Dad?" asked Tommy. "Where are you?" He blinked, confused, wiped his eyes. "Where'd my legs go?"

"I fixed you, Tommy," said Jon. "I fixed you."

"Dad—" said Tommy, staring at Jon, and Jon couldn't imagine what he saw.

"Look into my eyes, Tommy," said Jon. "Just look into my eyes."

Tommy did, staring at him, even as tears flowed from them.

"Remember, I love you, always," said Jon. "Okay?"

Tommy nodded. "I love you too," said Tommy.

"Take care of your mom," said Jon. "She won't let you, but do it anyway." Jon felt himself fading, he forced his eyes open, forced himself to look at Tommy.

"You're a good kid," said Jon. "Just do your best. I love you."

Jon's eyes closed, and no matter how hard he tried, they wouldn't open again. And then there was nothing.

31

Ten years later.

Tommy drove. The little electric car could go fast enough, and there was little traffic heading out into the country, even with all the construction.

"Fix America" was the new President's campaign slogan, and that's what they were doing, a nationwide effort to pave all the roads, shore up all the bridges, to restore the infrastructure of the country. Patterned after FDR's New Deal, it was working. Unemployment was down.

After a while he turned off the radio, and rolled down the windows, enjoying the soft summer breeze. Sure, it was warm, but the wind felt nice. He had the entire day, might as well enjoy it. The firm would be okay without him, even though there was a part that burned inside, that told him to work, work, work. Something he inherited from Dad, he guessed.

He admired the wind farms as he passed. They were still being built this time last year, but now they were up, churning at full speed, generating power. One of the rotors was his design, and he felt proud looking at them, whenever he spotted them. They'd be a part of the annual pilgrimage now, to visit his dad. Mom had stopped coming a few years back. He didn't blame her. It only made her sad. She had moved on, with a new husband. Tommy liked him.

Tommy pulled up to the gate, closed, and he swung it open, the metal creaking. Sweat beaded on his forehead, and he swiped at it with his sleeve. It was getting hotter every year, but their projections had it dropping again in a decade, if they continued. Not everything Shaw had developed down in the FUTURE lab was a weapon.

Tommy walked in a learned pattern, hitching every so often, but at a good pace. He didn't even need a cane. Sarah had finally convinced him to switch from the wheelchair. He had made the change for her and realized immediately he should have done it much sooner.

Tommy reached his dad, the gravestone marked with Jon's name, date of birth and death, and *Beloved Father* underneath.

Tommy sat down, the small bench nearby he had brought in a few years ago.

"Hi, Dad," said Tommy. "How are you?"

The wind whipped by, and grasshoppers sang in the background.

"I'm good," said Tommy. "I got promoted to junior partner in the firm. I told you about that rotor, right? Well, they used the design. But I'm not resting on my laurels. I'll be partner, sooner or later. They can't stop me."

Tommy paused.

"And I'm not overworking myself. I know, I know, it's in our blood. But I've been a lot better about limiting how much work I do. I had it out with Sarah, and she was right. She's always right. She always sees right through me. It's one of the reasons I love her. She doesn't put up with my bull-shit."

The grass swayed gently in the breeze, and the summer heat beat down on Tommy.

"I have some good news," said Tommy. "Sarah—Sarah is pregnant. She's due in a couple months. It's a boy," said Tommy. He felt a tear run down his cheek, and he wiped it away. "We're naming it Jonathan. Jon for short. Thought you would like that."

Tommy took a deep breath. "I think we're doing okay now, Dad. I mean, the world. Still a lot of problems, but maybe we're turning it around. I don't really know, but it seems better than it was. Fewer people starving, fewer people dying. That's probably as good a metric as any, right?"

The wind picked up, and Tommy felt a cool chill in the air. Thunder rumbled in the distance.

"Think it's going to rain. I should probably go. But it was nice to talk. I still love you, and I know you love me too." Tommy stood up on his prosthetic legs and reached into his pocket. He pulled out a small stone, rounded marble.

"That's from the yard, at our new house," said Tommy. "A little memento for you. I'll see you next year."

Tommy walked away.

Sign up for your free, exclusive novel!

Sign up for Robbie's newsletter! Monthly sneak peeks at upcoming projects, cover teases, and instant access to a free, exclusive novel!

www.robbiedorman.com/newsletter

Acknowledgements

Thank you to my wife Kim, for her patience and support. Thank you to my team of beta readers; Andrew, Matt, Megan, and Yousef, for your guidance and help. Thank you, for reading.

About the Author

Robbie Dorman believes in horror. Regrowth is his seventh novel. When not writing, he's podcasting, playing video games, or petting cats. He lives in Texas with his wife, Kim.

You can follow Robbie on Twitter @robbiedorman

CPSIA information can be obtained
at www.ICGtesting.com
Printed in the USA
LVHW031940160321
681694LV00006B/1353

9 781733 638869